THE '49 INDIAN

A Novel By

Craig Moody

www.vividimagerypublishing.com

Vivid Imagery Publishing paperback and digital first edition February 2017
Vivid Imagery Publishing hardcover first edition November 2018

Vivid Imagery Publishing books may be purchased in bulk for educational, business, fund-raising, or sales promotional use. For information, please e-mail Promotions@vividimagerypublishing.com.

Publishers Note: This book is a work of fiction. Any references to historical events, real people, or real places are used fictitiously. Other names, characters, places, and events are products of the author's imagination, and any resemblance to actual events or places or persons, living or dead, is entirely coincidental.

Cover art illustration by Gable Rynning
Cover art digital editing by Melissa Vespertine

Printed in the United States of America

ISBN 978-0-9986558-4-0 (Hardcover)
ISBN 978-0-9986558-1-9 (Paperback)
ISBN 978-0-9986558-2-6 (Kindle)
ISBN 978-0-9986558-3-3 (eBook)

THE '49 INDIAN

For Gable. Your love inspired this story and your presence anchored and energized me to write it. You have blessed my life in more ways than I could ever express. You are my Gauge.

To Mom, Tiffany, both Memas, and every single teacher, friend or relative who ever encouraged me to write. This is for you.

To Emmylou, Dolly, Madonna, and every artist whose lyrics have influenced and inspired me. Thank you.

And most of all and most importantly, to the Higher Power who blessed me with the calling to channel and deliver this gift of words and storytelling into the world, faithfully guiding me through each step of the process. I am forever grateful to be your humble steward.

His face was shaking, his body trembling. I wrapped my arms around him, choking back a sudden sob as he lifted both hands to cup my face. I opened my eyes to see the reflection of my expression staring back at me in the darkness of his gentle gaze, my brimming tears evident even in the shadowed closeness of our faces. I watched as my reflection fell from the black hole of his eyes and down the pinkness of his cheeks. The sob escaped me as he again pressed his lips to mine, our skin so close that the water of our eyes began to mingle like the confluence of two rivers.

I.

SUMMER

1983

THE FLORIDA SUN CARESSED MY SKIN AND BLINDED MY EYES as I strolled the Fort Lauderdale sidewalk. The slight summer breeze whistled atop my pores like lips over a bottle top. The muffled sounds of the constant traffic ebbed and flowed against the small bones of my ears, echoing its monotonous drone to the vacant corners of my mind. Cares and worries slipped from my focus like raindrops on a windshield, the brilliant summer day a rhythmic, slow-moving wiper of the brain. The fevered pace of my legs generated a pulsing dance of water upon my skin and a throbbing churn within my veins. A young man of twenty, I strolled along the street-side as confident as a king, yet naive as a toddler. The summer held its promise of adventure, my imagination wild with the possibilities of innocent mayhem and sinful passion. The whispered voice of my soul spoke gently of its intention, singing a song of the future wrapped in warmth within the familiar melody of my heart. The city skyline was not the only magnificent sight dominating the horizon. Beneath the confines of my mind, in the lairs that defied time and logic, a steadfast knowing of truth reverberated through my head like a gunshot fired in a canyon. This would be the summer my manhood would blossom. This would be the season I came to life.

Then, like a beacon rising from a desert mirage, I saw it. The building that had enslaved my curiosity for years. My mother called it a "den of sin"; my father would only scoff and grumble without saying a word, his judgment and assessment of the establishment clear and concise without verbal language. I, however, exploded with wonder. The shadowed sight of bare-chested men or cleverly disguised strangers ignited the limitless wick of my imagination like a stick of dynamite. It took me years to conjure the courage to simply entertain the possibility of walking near the place, much less venture inside. Today was it, though. I had planned this for months. It was time.

Pausing before the door like a weathered soul at the threshold of the afterlife, I stared in a paralysis of fear and disbelief. The years of imagining, the months of planning, my heart pounded so loudly inside my chest that I swore I could comprehend a meaning to its sound. Was it encouraging me to pull the handle? Was it screaming a drumming warning to turn and run? I didn't know, and for the first time in my life, I didn't care. There was no turning back now.

Grasping the enormous metal handle in my hand, I paused, swallowed, exhaled, and pulled with all my might. In an instant, the pungent sting of chlorine wrapped itself around my body. The glaring blast of the summer sun prevented my eyes from finding any form of vision beyond a black rectangle. My nose captured the striking smell as my ears absorbed the bass-heavy throb of disco music.

"Shut the door!" an irritated voice barked from within the darkness. As I quickly released my hand from its grip on the handle, the heavy door creaked and groaned in frustration, slamming its weight with force against my back. Like a poker chip being removed from the game, I slid into the lobby of the bathhouse as if placed there by some unseen force.

"Cash only," the voice continued, the identity behind it still mysterious in the darkness of the space. My sun-exposed eyes ached in their struggle to focus on the scene before me.

Slowly, the neon glow of the room came into view. Posters of half or fully naked men plastered the walls in a multi-layered wallpaper. The visual intensity of explicit sexuality fired across my brain in an unexpected blaze, its sensual effect trickling down my limbs like lava. Never in my life had I witnessed such a direct and blatant display of human sexuality, be it male or female. The countless images of exposed groins and erect male genitalia overwhelmed my cognizance to a point of near overload.

I jumped as the massive door re-exploded open behind me, the same blast of sunlight engulfing the tiny lobby in a brilliant sheet of white, breaking my hypnotic trance. A figure bumped my side as it passed, the unexpected human touch exhausting my courage and crippling my excitement. I turned to leave, when the same voice broke my movement.

"I can't have you blocking my doorway, kid," it snapped hastily. An awkward realization that I was now being watched by several pairs of eyes slowly began to drip over my flesh like warm July rain water. "You need to pay your entry and move along."

Like a moth to a flame, my body moved toward the voice in a stumbled shuffle. A window, covered with multicolored bars, stood between me and the source of my commander.

"$2.50. Cash only."

Coins began to bounce over the concrete floor as I fumbled in my jeans pockets for the funds. I could hear the voice sigh in frustration as I bent to retrieve the rogue quarters. Clumsily unfolding two one-dollar bills from their sweat-tinged, crumpled state, I placed the cash and coins onto the counter below the rainbow-colored bars. I was barely able to move my hand away, when a shadowed fist pulled the money into the darkness.

"Go ahead. Towel in the bin when you leave."

A buzzing screech, followed by a gunfire-like pop, signified the release of the door's lock. Anticipating the further disdain of the voice, I stepped toward the sound and reached into the dimly lit void until my hand secured a door knob. Gripping it, I twisted the metallic sphere until an exhaust of cold air assaulted my face. Taking a deep breath, I pushed the door as far as it would go, my shoes sliding onto a ceramic field of tiles. I now stood alone in a tiny corridor, the ominous buzz of the overhead florescent light bulbs protesting their labor to the chamber below. Allowing the door to slam shut behind me, I gathered my breath and permitted my feet to discover more of the tiled walkway. My eyes began to water as the acrid stench of chlorine filled my nostrils like a toxic gas. In the distance, the shuffling sounds of water and voices could be heard accenting the air of the space to come. The pulsating throb of the disco music seemed to capture my shoes and further my steps. It was as though each thud of the bass forced my movement into the darkness. I continued to creak across the humid-covered flooring, when a new voice broke my trance.

"Hey, baby, no one wants the mud tracks. You need to ditch the gear."

Nervously, I held my breath, unsure as to where the voice was coming from.

"Lockers are to your left."

Without hesitation, I turned my body to the left, sliding my shoes forward until they clicked the metallic wall of the promised lockers. My eyes began to focus as I quickly removed my shoes and jeans, rolling them into a ball and shoving them into one of the slender aluminum squares. I stood in a breathy silence until the same voice again invaded my stillness.

"Are you just gonna stand there in your shirt and briefs, or are you gonna drop trou and grab a towel like the rest of us?"

A short burst of laughter followed the words, the voice a sudden warm and semi-welcome sound.

"Towels are to your right, baby," the voice directed.

Assuming I was still being watched by the mysterious presence behind the ticket counter and fearing its scolding, I pulled my shirt above my head, quickly placing it with the rest of my garb. My heart raced as my fingers slipped beneath the elastic band of my briefs. Flickered images of my mother and father jumped before my eyes like some life-flashing vision one sees just before death. I felt my pulse skip and lurch as I slid the soft cotton down my thighs and to the floor. I nearly fell over as I pulled the undergarment from around my ankles.

Confidently tossing it with the rest of my clothing, I slammed the locker door shut and reached into the faint purple glow for a towel, white, stiff, rough, and ridged. I wrapped the towel around my waist and secured it as tightly as possible in the lower right corner of my abdomen. My pulse now deafened my hearing as I turned to face the stranger who lurked in the darkness behind me.

"Much better," the voice remarked as I took my first step forward, the slimy suction of my bare feet against the tile floor so slippery that I feared for my balance.

"I'm Eddie, by the way," the voice informed me as a hand slid down my lower back.

"Dustin," I choked, my voice cracking under the unexpected sound of my throat. Stating my name was the first audible sound I had made in hours.

"Glad you are here, Dustin," the voice continued, the hand now firmly gripped along the topside of my towel. "First time?"

"Yeah," I stumbled. "How can you tell?"

The voice burst into laughter as a dimly lit face slowly appeared in the faint glow of the fluorescents.

"Oh, it doesn't take a genius to figure that out, baby. You've got the look of a lamb wandering into a lion's den plastered all over that beautiful young face of yours."

I smiled, but my slight comfort was instantly broken by the forceful intrusion of the stranger's tongue against my own. Panicked, I pulled away, instinctively wiping my lips with my forearm.

"Oh, come on now," the voice laughed in a cough-heavy cackle. "I know you may look innocent, but you sure as hell know what goes on in this place."

He pulled the back of my towel, quickly leading me beyond the corridor and the lockers. Before I could speak or resist, we were in a tiny room, a small brown cot and a stool the only furniture I could clearly distinguish.

"Let me show you how it's done, Dustin."

With that said, the man snatched the towel from around my flesh, the cold, chlorine-heavy air now the only covering gracing my exposed nakedness.

"Mmm," the voice groaned before disappearing into the space below my hips.

Before I could utter a word, the man's mouth fully engulfed the entirety of my manhood. The warm sensation of his tongue caused my member to jump and pulse from the sudden entrapment.

"Eddie," I whispered, finding his head with my hands. "Please, Eddie. Stop."

With instant and extreme power, my hands were knocked from in front of me. The bones just below my lower forearms raced their message of pain to my brain. I opened my mouth to again protest, when I felt the force of his enclosed fist repeatedly meeting the tender skin around my left eye.

"Shut the fuck up, little faggot!"

The voice was now in my face, the twisted and gnarled expression just inches from my nose.

"This is what you came here for!"

The man stuck his bare foot between my own, pulling it back and knocking me to the floor. Gripping a fistful of my hair, he pulled my head upward, my throat too stretched for me to vocalize. My breath deflated from my lungs as he launched his knee into the center of my spine. My hands slid from their crawl-like position and toward the wall. I could feel the rattled clack of my teeth as my upper and lower jaw impacted the ceramic plane of the floor. The pain was immediately forgotten as the press of the man's hips lowered my buttocks to the ground. I cried out in agony as he forcefully entered my body, the invasion of his appendage an excruciating burning. His fist slammed my mouth before I could cry out again.

My head pounded against the solid wall as Eddie thrust his pelvis into mine. The taste of his fisted fingers pressed tightly against my teeth was that of cigarettes and pool water. The flashed images of my mother and father again appeared across the film screen behind my eyes, on an endless, tormenting loop. What I wouldn't give to simply fall into the scenes that flickered over the darkness behind my lids. The love, the safety, the security of their comforting presence, all a stark contrast to the nightmarish reality I now found myself in. Tears streamed down my skin and onto Eddie's hands. I could taste their salt-heavy presence as they soaked his fists.

"Fuck!" he screamed, lifting my face from the floor with a handful of my hair. "Fuck!"

He continued his chant, his body convulsing under the strained cry of each outburst.

"Fuck! Fuck! Fuck!"

Then, as quickly as it had begun, it was over. Eddie released my hair, my head falling with a solid thud to the cold, moist floor. I wasn't sure if I was breathing. I didn't know if my eyes were open or closed. All I knew was that it was over.

A cold and nearly lifeless body on the floor, I did not move as I felt the man lift himself from behind me. The feel of his wet skin unsticking itself from mine was the only sensation I could mentally compute and physically recognize.

I felt his presence looming above me, his breathing hard and shallow. Clearing his throat, I heard him summon mucus from his upper chest, lifting it from the hollows and across the open cavern of his mouth like a cannon, the sound of his spit a weighted bullet as it splattered across my lower back.

"Fuckin' faggot."

His insult fell to the floor as heated and hateful as his saliva. I lay in silence as I felt him swoop his towel from the ground and wrap it around his waist. He paused, cleared his throat again, hurled the wet contents onto my backside, and then exited the room.

I didn't move for what felt like hours. My breath continued on its own, my heart sounding its pulsing drum in my ears like a tribal war cry. The constant ache of my lower body was the only evidence I held for my continued physical existence. Despite the circumstantial chaos, my mind was still, my ego silent. The quiet voice of my soul assured me of my well-being, though I could still sense its weeping.

Slowly, I began to move, lifting my body from the floor as if it were fractured glass. I felt myself rise into the darkened space which had floated above me like a poisonous gas, inundating my lungs and stinging my face. I didn't care where the towel was. I simply moved my hands along the slime-like texture of the walls until I found the small door. Pushing it open, I gasped as the cooler and slightly familiar air of the hallway entered my body. Stumbling, I slid my feet along the dimly lit corridor until I reached the locker area. Fumbling through the haze that surrounded my eyes, I somehow located my clothing within the first locker that I tried.

Tossing the garments onto my body without thought or care, I shoved my feet into my shoes and limped to the exit. It was then that I felt the warm, thick sensation running down the back of my legs. Pausing, I slid my hand into the rear of my jeans and toward my inner thighs. Returning the hand to my face, my heart skipped and stuttered as the unmistakable crimson stain of blood found recognition within my brain.

Pressing the bloodstained hand onto the door, I erupted into the lobby as if escaping a life-sentence prison term. The still unseen voice of the ticket booth shouted something in anger as I clumsily stormed through the entryway. The blinding light of the street stunned my senses as I fell onto the sidewalk. The heavy metal door of the bathhouse slammed behind me like the echoing roar of a medieval dungeon. Then, the world went black.

***

I AWOKE TO THE sound of hospital machinery whirring and beeping around my head. Slowly opening my eyes, I toured the room with blurry vision, taking in the scene before me. A faded peach color adorned the medical-equipment-heavy walls. A large television set murmured in the corner. A balloon and flowers accented the table at the foot of the bed. My mother sat beside me.

"Mom," I whispered, my voice dry and cracked.

My vision cleared as I watched the face of my mother absorb the site of me, a nervous wariness dominating her expression.

"Dustin," she whispered, her voice breathless and worried. "My baby boy."

Our hands locked. Instantly, a warm feeling of protection blanketed over me.

"Oh, Mom."

Squeezing her hand tighter, I didn't attempt to stop the flood of tears that began to stream down my face. The vivid memory of what had occurred danced through my mind like a demon on the shores of the lake of fire. The smell of the chlorine, the stark coldness of the tile floor, the smell of Eddie's breath, even the feel of his skin next to mine, it all surrounded me as if finding its way from the recent past and into the present. I began to sink deeper into the memory, when my mother's voice broke the nightmarish trance.

"The police told me that they found you on the sidewalk," her voice quivered, the obvious stress of the ordeal still heavy on her heart. "What happened, dear?"

She didn't say it, but I knew the question that was to come next. More than likely, the police had also mentioned just where on the sidewalk they had found me and the establishment it was in front of. I prepared myself for the inevitable interrogation.

"They said they found you outside of a building, Dustin," she continued, an obvious strain hovering over her words as she attempted to control her emotions. "Do you know what sort of building it was?"

I could only glare at her, half in physical pain and half in disbelief that my own mother wasted not one second at satiating her need for control. Even the police had yet to question me.

"A bathhouse, Dustin," she replied flatly, obviously uninterested in any reply. "A gay bathhouse. What were you doing in front of that place?"

I watched as her motherly gaze of concern melted into a stare of fear and rage.

"Answer me, Dustin."

I didn't know what to say. She didn't have proof that I was in the bathhouse, yet she was positive that I was. Every fiber of my being could feel her angered certainty. It felt as though she were only seconds from pouncing from the chair and onto the bed, physically exhausting her obvious discontent onto my body. I swallowed and held my breath as the words began to form just beneath my quivering lips. Before I could speak, the door to the room burst open, revealing the chatter of the hallway beyond and the presence of my father. In his hand was another balloon, this one far larger and more colorful than the first.

"Hey, son!" he exclaimed, his face beaming with relief as he closed the door behind him and quickly made his way to my bedside. "I am so glad to see you awake, my boy."

A rush of relief and sorrow melted over me as I felt my father wrap his arms around my shoulders. He pressed his head onto my face, the smell of his hair and skin a lifetime familiarity. Beneath the chatter of the hospital machinery, I could hear him softly sobbing.

"Hey, Dad," I choked, my voice drier and more sore than before. "I'm okay."

I caught a glimpse of my mother through the intertwinement of my father's arms, her expression frozen and terrified. I could tell it was taking every bit of inner strength she could muster not to burst out with her continued line of questioning.

"Your mother and I have been worried sick, son. You have been in here for hours."

It was then that I noticed the lack of sunlight beyond the hospital window. It was obvious that a vast chunk of time had passed since my last conscious memory.

"I brought you some food," my father announced, quickly moving to the corner of the room.

I kept my eyes glued to his back, the burning sizzle of my mother's glare searing into my skin like a laser. I managed a nervous, dry gulp, which taunted the piercing thirst of my throat. I kept my gaze centered on my father, absolutely terrified to even casually glance at my mother.

"Here we go," my father boasted cheerfully, displaying a massive hoagie on the tray before me. "I just picked it up from Sub Center, so it's good and fresh."

I stared at the sandwich as if glimpsing a humane form of sustenance for the first time after being stranded on a deserted island for years. I didn't know if I should simply admire its existence or scarf it down like a stray dog discovering a chicken bone with a bit of cold, cooked flesh still attached.

"We should tell the detective that he is awake," my mother stated flatly, her stare still fixed on me yet her words directed at my father.

I watched as my hands collected the hoagie and lifted it from the wax paper it rested on. Saliva began to pool beneath my tongue as the oversized sandwich neared my starving mouth.

"We should let him eat and get some more rest before we do that, Teresa," my father replied, busily tying the latest balloon to the foot of the bed.

"No, Nathan," she shot back immediately. "They asked us to contact them the moment he came to. The boy is a victim of an attack, and I am not just going to sit here idly while—"

"Okay, okay," my father whispered, interrupting my mother's plea with his arms. I watched in silence as my parents embraced, the sheer terror of their energy as palpable as the hoagie to my now satiated taste buds.

My mother stood from her chair, wiping her eyes with the sleeve of her sweater as she made her way to the door. She didn't hesitate or look back as she frantically exited the room. The blast of cold air from the hallway shot through me like a cannonball as she closed the door firmly behind her.

"You have to forgive your mom, son," my dad stated, breaking the sudden silence. "She is just scared out of her mind."

He leaned closer, the unmistakable scent of his cologne aftershave wafting under my nostrils like a welcome spring breeze over a wintered field.

"You are still her baby boy, you know."

I closed my eyes as my father gently pressed his open hand over my cheek. The touch of his skin seemed to cool and extinguish the sputtered flames of trauma and stress that still burned inside me. A tear escaped one of my sealed eyelids, slowly inching its way down my upper cheek and onto my father's weathered hand. The moment seemed to suspend time as I focused on the sensations the simple touch conjured within me.

The cannon-like blast of the hallway air again flooded the space around me as my mother reentered the room, this time, a burly man in a brown corduroy suit trailing her fevered pace.

"This is Detective Sherman," she breathlessly declared, her words shaken yet firm. "He is here to ask you some questions."

I looked at my father, who still stood beside me, his expression worried and uncertain by the sudden appearance of the detective. I returned my slow gaze to the stranger, taking in his stern appearance the same way a kitten curiously paws at a lizard.

The man stood tall, his dark brown hair slicked back, a bushy mustache accenting his upper lip. His eyes matched the color of his hair, his glare as glazed and hard as the matted brown helmet atop his scalp. A bit of some form of pastry clung lifelessly to the lower right corner of his impressively thick mustache, its volume and bulk reaching at least a half an inch from his skin. He was both attractive and odd, his appearance both enticing and nerve-wracking.

"It is good to see you awake, Mr. Thomas," the detective stated, his expression motionless and controlled. "I know your parents have been very worried."

He nodded toward each of my parents as he spoke, pausing for what appeared to be a calculated attempt at genuine concern and sympathy, and then returned his expression to its unmoving resting place.

"I have some questions that I am going to need to ask you, Mr. Thomas," his voice now stronger and more direct than before. "Some of these questions may make you uncomfortable, so I will understand if you would like to ask your parents to leave the room while we talk."

Unsure how to respond, I could only stare at the detective. My pulse began to quicken as my imagination contemplated the possible questions he was about to ask. With my breath now shallow and stuttered, I swallowed hard and looked at my parents. My father nodded slightly before approaching my mother. He placed his hands softly on her shoulders and pulled her toward him. I could see my mother hesitate. Her need to be involved and inevitably control the situation was overwhelming her. Still, she followed my father's lead and exited the room.

"Now," Detective Sherman began, clearing his throat and pulling a small notepad from his jacket pocket.

I was amused at how comically accurate his appearance, demeanor, speech, and actions were to that of the stereotypical police detectives I saw on television. The only elements missing were a cigarette and an obnoxious theme song.

"I need you to recount for me every detail of what occurred at the bathhouse, son," he continued, flipping the pages of his small, worn notebook to what I assumed was a blank page.

I watched as he struggled to find his pen, it too tucked deep within the labyrinth of his inner coat.

"I need for you to be explicitly accurate, Dustin. Every single detail is vital if we are going to locate your perpetrator."

My heart was deafening now. It felt as though the blood-pounding organ had somehow relocated itself into the confines of my skull, pushing my brain down into the hollows of my inner core, replacing my thoughts with its pulsating beat.

"Let's go, Dustin," Detective Sherman commanded impatiently. "I can't be here all night."

"Okay," I started, my words falling into the room as broken and heavy as the Titanic descending into the abyss.

The detective didn't react or pause as he carefully listened and scribbled onto his pad. It was as if he already knew the entire story before I told it. Nothing seemed to faze him, not even the violently explicit details of the assault.

"Mr. Thomas," Detective Sherman sighed after I concluded my statement, flipping his notebook shut and replacing it with the pen into his jacket. "Do your parents know that you are a homosexual?"

The question paralyzed my heart. The feeling of the beating organ's presence in my head sank back down into my hollow chest cavity. I was holding my breath, frightened and unsure as to how to reengage my lungs.

"Son," he continued, my hesitation the obvious answer to his question, "I am only asking you this because I am trying to figure out a way to inform them of the details without causing some sort of upset or friction between you."

He paused a moment, taking in what I assumed was my horrified expression before closing his eyes.

"Dustin, your personal business is not the focus of this investigation. You were attacked and sexually assaulted, and that is the crime that has been committed. Not your sexual orientation."

I felt my lungs fill and then collapse under the sudden arrival of the detective's reassurance. A warm, comforting wave crashed over my body as I realized the conversation I dreaded and feared most in my entire life was not about to take place as I lay helpless in a hospital bed.

"I am going to bring your parents back in," he announced, moving to the door. "I will call them in a few days. When I do, I am telling them that the investigation will require more interviewing. I plan to speak with some of thebathhouse employees and other patrons. I will not disclose anything further."

He stared at me cautiously before turning the doorknob.

"What you decide to tell them is up to you."

With that said, he pulled the door completely open, nearly spilling my mother into the room.

"Mrs. Thomas," Detective Sherman nodded, his expressionless stare unbroken.

I watched in silence as the detective exited the room while my father and mother rushed back inside like two eager cattle returning to the barn to feed.

"Well?" my mother asked, resuming her position next to the bed. "What did he say?"

I could only stare back at her, uncertain as to how to form any words.

"Dustin?" she continued, her look of concern fading into impatience and frustration.

"Dear," my father said softly, approaching her from behind. "The boy has been through so much. Let's just leave him be for now. The police will do their job."

My mother snapped her head at him as though he had just blasphemed the name of Christ.

"How dare you tell me to relax!" she shot. "This is my child we are speaking of. My child who was found outside of a...a..."

Her words faded into an insecure void, her angered expression falling with it.

"He said they were going to interview some of the witnesses nearby," I stated with confidence. "There were some. Witnesses. On the street. They saw me get attacked."

My parents simply stared at me, a whirlwind of thoughts and emotions obvious through the windows of their loving eyes.

"There," my father replied, gripping my mother's tense shoulders with both of his hands. "The police are going to take care of this, darling. I promise you."

My mother could only stare, her eyes spiraling in a mix of colors fueled by confusion, suspicion, and rage. She knew there was more to the story, and I knew she would not rest until she got it from me.

"Fine," she stated flatly. "Fine."

She took her place in the seat next to my bed and began fumbling through her purse. My father patted my knee, smiling at me as though I had just managed an unlikely win at some Boy Scout sport competition.

Slowly, either from the medication dripping into my veins or absolute mental and emotional exhaustion, I slipped beyond the darkness behind my eyes and into a deeply peaceful sleep.

***

IT HAD BEEN EXACTLY one month since the attack. There was no word from the police. No calls, no visits. Only silence. I didn't mind, as I would rather not relive the details of that day, but my mother was slowly teetering on the edge of her already frayed emotional ledge. Nearly every dinner conversation reverted to the subject, usually ending with my mother berating my father for not being more proactive by harassing the police or Detective Sherman on a daily basis. I never contributed to the conversation. I would only lock my gaze onto my delicate dinnerplate and wait for the discussion to meet its usual end.

Other than that, my life was slowly returning to its paralyzed state of normality. Without falter, the common summer days slipped in and out of my existence like grains of sand blowing on the beachside. Aside from the trauma of my bathhouse visit, absolutely nothing of importance or worth any sort of memory-capture transpired. My life had become an endless cycle of flipping through comic books, skimming my mother's massive collection of tacky romance novels, and hours of staring at pointless daytime television. Besides the occasional telephone call from my cousin Ruby in Tennessee,

I had limited contact or communication with anyone outside of my parent's house. Slowly each day, I could feel my boredom seep beyond the fading limits of my spirit and into the inner depths of my soul. A part of me was secretly fantasizing about how much better it would have been to have never woken up in that hospital bed after the attack.

"Mom!" I yelled into the distance of the house beyond the foyer. "I'm gonna go ride my bike."

Silence.

I turned to the front door and began to make my exit when I heard my mother's post-nap vocals echo down the stairway.

"Don't go past the cul-de-sac," she croaked, her voice soggy yet parched from slumber. "And be home when the streetlights come on."

I slammed the door behind me, irritated and annoyed that her response to my bike riding at age twenty was no different than it had been when I was only eight.

As I moved in the direction of the garage, the full view of the street opened beyond the manicured hedges of our lawn. Neighbors peppered the scenery as I strolled toward the side of the house where my bike was stored. It was clear that the soft, warm Florida evening breeze had lured the residents from their caverns of air-conditioned shelter, where they hibernated from the extreme midday heat. I closed my eyes and inhaled deeply, allowing the warm, humidity-thick wind to swirl and align my lungs. Exhaling, I opened my eyes, my vision clearing but my heart ceasing to beat.

I stood in complete silence as my body began to adjust to the sight it was viewing. Raven-haired, glistening skin, a myriad of colorful tattoos adorning the arms, a gorgeous human male glided past the hedges, the sound of a gas-powered lawnmower leading the way. My heart found its pace, jumping from what felt like complete stillness to a racing, deafening pound. My breathing shallowed as the summer wind I had only recently captured now expelled and fled back into the air around me. I could only stare, my gaze transfixed and bewildered.

I watched as he reappeared and then disappeared behind the limited view of the hedges. He moved methodically, focused and dedicated to his laborious chore, oblivious to my trance-like presence.

Catching myself, I moved to my bicycle, pulling it from its place behind my father's meticulously lined gardening tools, and hopped onto the seat. Peddling frantically for the street, I kept my eyes trained on the sidewalk before me, excited yet terrified to gain a closer look at the mysterious lawn man.

Rounding the corner of the hedges, I watched in unexpected horror as my bike's front tire slammed into a person's pant leg.

"Sorry!" I shouted, absorbing my shock and looking up toward my victim's face. "I didn't mean to—"

It was him, the mysterious lawn man, shirtless and glowing like a 1940s film star.

"Hey, man, it's okay," a voice boomed, its depth and power vibrating the airwaves around me.

I watched as my reflection slipped and fell into the darkness of his pupils. It was then and there that I lost myself.

"I'm Gauge," the voice continued, a hand reaching up from the distance below his waist. "This is my aunt's new place. We just moved in last week."

I could only stare, my voice completely frozen and locked beneath the now tense flesh of my throat. Instinctively, I too reached out my hand, my blood racing in my veins as my skin connected with his.

"I'm Dustin."

"Nice to meet ya, Dustin," he replied, a crooked smile tugging at the right side of his mouth. His eyes sparkled as he reached behind his back, retrieving an old white rag, lifting it to his sweat-covered forehead. His soft face, a mix of Elvis Presley and a young Marlon Brando, I watched in a dreamlike haze as he ran the cloth over his skin. Never in my entire life had the presence of another human being ignited and hypnotized each of my senses, heightening their awareness. I could feel the heat from his bare flesh and smell the tinge of musk and sweat that draped over him like a sun-beaten cloak. As if seeing for the very first time, I allowed my eyes to tour every inch of his being. His faded blue jeans fit tight around his legs, the curvature of his natural muscle tone accentuated by the perfect grip of the denim. Enamored, or simply overtaken by pure lustfulness, I felt each and every one of my muscles, limbs, ligaments, and bones gravitate toward him. It was as though some unseen force was pulling me from the inside out and into his inner core.

"So, you live around here, Dustin?" he asked, replacing the rag to its holding place in his right-rear jean pocket. Blood raced to the surface of my cheeks as my eyes followed his hand's movement to his backside. My heart skipped and fumbled as it struggled to find its pace. I cleared my throat under the weight of my sudden nervousness and forced my overstimulated attention back to his eyes. Immediately, I tumbled headfirst into his reflective gaze, the darkness that offset the white an endless tunnel I willingly and fearlessly journeyed into.

"Yes," I replied weakly, my voice now chapped and stressed by the pressure of my cyclonic emotions. "I live right here."

I felt his attention follow my voice as I nodded over my shoulder in the direction of my parents' picturesque Americana showcase home. With my head still turned, my lungs froze as the corner of my eye caught his gaze return to me.

"Wow, nice," he added, smiling. "Great neighborhood."

I watched as his dark eyes slowly scanned the street before returning their focus to me. The moment I felt them move across my face, as the moon glides its reflective watch over the tide, my entire body shivered and trembled. Like the thirst of the sea, I felt as though I could savor this moment for eternity.

"Well," he broke the silence, his voice booming through the stillness like an ancient cannonball barreling through the air. "I better get back to it. My aunt will have my ass if this lawn ain't perfect by sunset."

Another pause, the Florida breeze cutting the space between us like angels cloaking their allotted children.

"It was nice to meet ya, Dustin."

Gauge's hand was warm and wet. The sensation of his sweat lingered on my palm as he pulled his grip from the handshake.

"Feel free to pop over sometime," he continued. "My aunt makes a mean banana pudding. She'd love it if I invited a new neighbor over for a visit."

I stood silent and speechless, my ability to speak seemingly lost and forgotten. After what felt like a century, I was finally able to break my voice's frozen stillness and croak out a pathetic jumble of polite gratitude.

Then, as quickly as he had appeared, Gauge dashed behind the hedges and back onto the half-cut landscape of the lawn.

My heart throbbed and pounded inside my head as I tossed my leg over the bicycle seat and rode into the street. A golden haze fogged my vision as I pedaled, uncertain as to the goal or direction of my ride. My thighs began to ache as I feverishly cycled into the unknown, thoughts and images failing to sway my mind to their obsessive calling. Instead, only the smooth face of Gauge, his piercing yet warm eyes, along with the bass-heavy echo of his voice, dominated my brain.

The buzzing flicker of the streetlights slowly pulled my attention back into the now. The oversized living room window of Gauge's aunt's house revealed the contents of her still unpacked home, boxes towering the visible areas like the skyscrapers of Manhattan. I glided past, no sign of Gauge or his aunt, rounded the hedges and back to the side of the house where my bike was kept.

As I reentered the house, the familiar aroma of one of my mother's common dinner meals wafted into my nostrils, replacing the still lingering sweetness of Gauge's skin and sweat.

The stairway felt like Jell-O as I bounded its casing to the second floor. My mother's voice sounded like a droned warble as I burst through the doorway of my room, landing on my bed as cumbersome and heavy as a steel ship launching into the harbor for the very first time. I rolled into the corner and pulled the blankets above my head. Again and again, the meeting with Gauge replayed inside my mind like an old filmstrip stuck on a projector wheel. I watched and re-watched the same scene over and over until my consciousness surrendered to slumber.

The sound of the mysterious boy's voice provided the melody of my dreams while the slick shine of his perspiring skin aroused and provoked a surge of ecstasy.

***

THREE DAYS HAD PASSED since I last saw Gauge. Still, the memory of our meeting dominated my thinking. Each moment of the day was somehow rooted in my awareness of him. I found myself compulsively checking out the windows of the house that could view his aunt's yard. Each day, my heart sank as another sun rose and set without a brief glimpse of the person who had ignited my senses like no other. I felt tortured and taunted, like a sea-bound refugee discovering an abandoned canteen, only to savor one last isolated drop of fresh water while stranded atop the salt-laced tears of the ocean. My nights always ended the same, a furious series of rounds of self-pleasure with Gauge's touch and smell the guiding focus of my unprecedented arousal. Never in my life had my ability to fantasize caused my entire physical being to tremble and convulse in response. My routine and immature self-release had morphed and evolved into a powerful ritual of solo lovemaking. The depth of my sleep after each climax rivaled that of a newborn infant.

I no longer thought of my attack. It wasn't that I no longer cared, it was a simple case of perception refocusing. The overwhelming sensual enormity I felt after meeting Gauge slipped my brain into an ongoing dance of fantasy and obsession. I wasn't even annoyed or bothered by my mother's relentless and useless recycling of the topic each night at the dinner table. Even my father appeared to completely tune her out. Perhaps his brain was venturing back to a time when my mother was more gentle and simplistic. Or perhaps he used these intense and uncomfortable dinner discussions to slip into an alternate dream world where the only voice he had to endure was his own...or Suzanne Somers's.

"Dustin!"

My mother's impatient voice penetrated my spiraling mindlessness like a bullet shattering glass.

"I have asked you to take the trash out twice already."

I raised my eyes to meet hers, a mixture of annoyance and sympathy defining her expression.

"Do not make me ask you a third time."

Lifting myself from the dinner table, I gathered my plate and utensils and carried them to the kitchen. Placing them gently into the pristine porcelain sink, I moved to the trash can and gathered the overstuffed contents. Escaping the kitchen through the side door that led to the garage, I rounded the corner of the house and froze.

It took me a moment to decipher if my vision was simply still attached to my daylong fantasizing or if I was actually taking in the tangible sight of Gauge. He was squatting beside an antique-looking motorcycle, the bit of skin revealed between his T-shirt and jeans exposing the elastic rim of white Fruit of the Loom briefs. I felt my pulse and penis react to the site in a simultaneous jolt. I suddenly became awkward and nervous about what to do. Placing the trash bag into the tin garbage can that rested alongside the garage would certainly attract Gauge's attention, something I both craved and dreaded with equal intensity.

Before I had the chance to decide my move, Gauge rose to his full height and threw his leg over the bike. I watched in a heart-pounding silence as he kick-started the motor. I struggled to breathe as I viewed him lift a worn-out black helmet from behind him and place it onto his head. His fingers moved effortlessly and smoothly as he slid the strap under his chin and through the small brass buckle. Then, he looked directly at me.

I wasn't quite sure if my heart stopped beating or if my lungs collapsed. The sudden connection with his eyes left me stunned and senseless. Every cell of my being was now connected to his gaze.

He motioned for me to approach him.

Somehow, my feet obliged. I dropped the trash bag into the tin garbage bin and started to move. I struggled to catch my breath as I unconsciously approached him. The small distance between the trash can and his bike was mere feet, but felt like the light years between Earth and a neighboring galaxy. It was as if some other unseen presence was lifting and lowering my legs. I choked back a dried wad of nervous terror as the space between us closed into a ruler's worth of inches.

"Get on!" he shouted over the grumbling growl of the motorcycle's obviously aged and worn engine.

I tilted my head in confusion, half in genuine misunderstanding and half in a pulse-racing surge of excitement.

I pointed at my scalp.

"What about a helmet?" I shouted, leaning in toward his ear.

He nodded, paused, and then lifted his head back and unbuckled the straps under his chin. His dark hair fell to the side as he pulled the black object into the air. I closed my eyes as he gently placed it on top of my uncombed and careless mane. The touch of his fingers as he maneuvered the straps and buckle electrified my skin, delivering a current of adrenaline coated in disbelief and anticipation. Peering through a small slit in my eyes, my breath shook and shivered as I watched him bite the corner of his lip in focused concentration. My mind hesitated as I realized the simple placement of his nibbling teeth and pink lip was now the most erotic image I had ever seen.

"Come on," Gauge commanded as he ensured the fastened seal of the strap.

Without hesitation, I climbed aboard the motorcycle. My feet were bare, my summer shorts and worn nightshirt my only clothing. I gripped my hands onto Gauge's broad shoulders, the warmth of his skin vibrant and radiating just below the soft cloth of his T-shirt.

"No!" I heard him shout above the throttling engine. "Here."

He reached behind him and lowered one of my arms to his waist. Understanding his movement, I met both hands at the center of his core. I was certain my heart would leap from its bone cage prison deep within my chest.

"You good?" he asked, turning his head to the left so that his ear could hear my response.

"Yeah," I struggled to project over the now revving groan of the motorbike's engine. "I'm on."

I felt him lift the bike into balance, kick in the clutch, and turn the throttle. Within seconds, we were halfway down the street and gliding past the single stop sign that divided our neighborhood from the busier city road. I didn't think to notify my parents of my leaving or to ask Gauge where it was we were going. I simply leaned my chest against the warm plane of his back and just rode.

***

WE RODE FOR WHAT must have been half an hour, sweeping through endless side streets and residential shortcuts until we entered the Florida Everglades. Palm trees and sawgrass cut the glimmer from the fading sunset as we grumbled over a dirt road and into the coming night. Gauge switched on the bike's single headlight as the density of the surrounding foliage thickened and threatened the remaining natural visibility. I was amazed at how serene and calm I was. My body had become accustomed to the feel of Gauge just beneath my heartbeat. I no longer struggled to stay mindful of my breathing or racing pulse. Instead, I simply allowed myself to rest easy against him, just riding in silence into the unknown.

I lifted my head as Gauge turned the bike down an adjacent trail and toward what appeared to be a large body of water. Within seconds, the reflective surface of a lake slid into view as the motorcycle echoed from beneath the trees and onto the lake bed. The tires were nearly touching the water when Gauge finally gripped the brake and cut the engine. I lifted my face toward the sky and into the brilliant site of a full moon glowing brightly within an endless canvas of pinkish purple. The faded glow of countless stars began to flicker to life underneath the weakening smolder of the slowly forgotten sun. Without the distraction of city lights, I was breathless at how vivid the night was. Even when Gauge clicked the headlight off, I could still clearly see every facet and feature of the earth that surrounded us. Each rock formation and palmetto plant was detailed in the darkness as though lit from within by some natural light source. The mirror-like stillness of the lake reflected the moon into the space above it, creating a near spotlight of visibility. In my twenty years of life, I was certain I had never witnessed such a truly spectacular night sky.

"This," Gauge broke the silence with his deep and booming voice, "is my favorite place on the planet."

He paused, his face a cool shade of blue, illuminated by the giant pool of water that began just inches from his feet.

"My dad used to bring me here when I was a kid."

He turned to me, his dark eyes twinkling like the now brilliant stars above us.

"This was his bike."

He patted the leather seat with his hand. I slid off the back and stood beside him. It was as if the carefully constructed vehicle of chrome, metal, and rubber had inhaled a breath of life and was now its own being.

The shift in Gauge's energy revealed a wealth of answers to questions my mind had yet to ask. Without him speaking further, I was somehow certain that his father was no longer alive.

"It's a '49 Indian," Gauge continued, his voice lifting from his obvious emotional distraction. "I rebuilt the engine myself."

I watched as he squatted to the side of the cooling motor.

"It isn't 100 percent yet, but she gets me where I need to be."

I remained still and quiet as I watched him glide his gaze across the dimly lit side of the bike. In an unspoken confirmation between us, it was as though the soul of his father had somehow embodied the classic motorcycle. Gauge didn't speak as he ran his hand slowly down the faded maroon of the bike's front fender. I only knew him a combination of mere minutes, yet I clearly understood that he was now somehow connecting with his dad, a man who I was certain, but had no confirmation of, was no longer sharing the air of this planet.

"Pop has been gone a year," Gauge confirmed softly, as if reading the energy of my thoughts. "Cancer. Took him out in less than a year. Fucking cigars."

The rawness of his vulnerability was as startling as it was comforting. In a silent yet understood way, I instantly felt I had known this man for as many years as my heart had been beating. Something told me that Gauge felt the same. For the first time that I could recall, I was truly alive in the present moment.

"We used to come camping here."

He stood up, turning his body back toward the water.

"It was always my favorite thing to do with him."

I held my breath as I heard his voice quiver slightly.

"Pop was good, Dustin. He was a good man."

A star fell from its place among the gathering of its fellow ancestors. The reflection of its descent on the water made the poetic sight all the more visible and suspended in time. I felt as if I were alive in some lucid dream. I lifted my fingers to my arm, tugging the light hairs to be sure I could still feel them.

"Come on," Gauge declared excitedly, lifting his shirt above his head.

I couldn't blink as I watched him strip down to his briefs, the bleached cleanliness of the material absorbing the moonlight like an evening primrose. My brain struggled to process what it was seeing. Flashed images of my pre-sleep fantasies of the last few nights flickered across the screen of my mind like a filmstrip breaking free of a projector reel. A flash of white shot across my field of vision before my pupils widened and hyper-focused onto the unbelievable sight before me. I stood lifeless as I observed the pale posterior of Gauge's backside appear from the darkness.

Like the moon above us, the rounded curvature of his rear beamed and glowed against the blackness that surrounded it. I watched in a pulsating trance as he splashed the water and faded into the distance of the reflective pool beyond.

"Come on, man!" he shouted back toward me, his face lit clearly by the reflection of the moonlit water.

Slowly, I began to move, lifting my pajama shirt above my head, its worn softness still carrying the aroma of my mother's homemade pepper-roasted chili. Tossing it over the back of the motorcycle's giant leather seat, I jumped as my bare skin began to touch the unexpected coolness of the water.

"No!" Gauge yelled, laughing. "You can't get your clothes wet, man. You gotta get down to the skin!"

I imagined that my now red-hot face had to be glowing like a cattle prod recently pulled from a flame. An overwhelming feeling of sheer disbelief draped over my bare shoulders as thick and heavy as the swampy humidity that engulfed the Florida night. It was as if the gods above had heard my silent prayer, whispered deep within the frenzied fervor of my recent fantasies, and delivered my unspoken plea into existence.

Slowly, in a collective movement, I lowered my worn summer shorts and faded blue briefs from their comfortable grip around my waist. The sensation of the naked summer air atop my skin was dense and cumbersome, as if falling into a fresh mud patch after a long summer rain.

Immediately, I plunged into the water, dropping my body below the surface as quickly as was humanly possible. The fact that Gauge was witness to my nudity was embarrassing yet endlessly exciting. Without thought, I swam toward him, joining his slow kicking beyond the grassy shallows of the lake.

"Well done, my friend," Gauge teased as I neared him. "Butt-ass naked is the only way to swim as far as I'm concerned."

He smiled, the crooked grin chiseled across his youthful face as warm and inviting as a freshly baked apple pie. My heart skipped in its rhythm as I found myself lost in his care-free expression.

"Too bad the folks down at the community pool don't agree."

He watched my face, anticipating a reaction before bursting into an authentic fit of his own laughter. I wasn't sure if I was laughing too or simply staring, the enormity of emotion that surrounded me as sealed as the lake water's seamless grip across every inch of my bare flesh.

"So, my new neighbor, Dustin," he stated, gathering his voice from the exhausted spiral of his laughter. "Tell me about yourself. Who is this mysterious person I am swimming butt-ass naked with?"

For the first time in my life, I was truly speechless. I didn't know what to say. The unbelievable reality of the present was so overwhelming and surreal that my brain seemed to have lost its ability to form words and thoughts, much less express a relevant and coherent understanding of who I was as a person. In truth, I wasn't quite sure if even I knew who I was anymore. Alive in this moment, I felt born again. The sudden events of the past few days had ignited something within me that I was unfamiliar with yet soulfully aware of. It was almost as if that first encounter with Gauge had flipped some unseen switch, an inner gear that was shifted from a careful, casual coasting, to a dangerous, speeding acceleration.

"Well," I began, my voice cracking from the weight of my nerves, "I was born and raised here. In that house...the house you saw."

I felt myself growing more tense and red beneath the grandeur of the sailing silver moon.

"I live there with my folks. No brothers or sisters or anything."

I watched as Gauge eagerly absorbed my words, the reflection of my face within the darkness of his eyes vibrant and three dimensional.

"We don't even have a dog or anything."

I felt so stupid. My words fell from my mouth as clumsily and uncertain as a baby giraffe standing and walking for the very first time. Still, I could feel Gauge's interest pulling and tugging at my brain like a curious toddler, fully focused and present in the world that surrounded him.

"Cool, man," he replied cheerfully when my fumbling words ceased to continue. "I was born here too. Only, my folks didn't stay together. My mom took off when I was just a lil' tyke, and my dad bounced me around with him till the cancer took him."

His eyes faded into the shallows as the shimmering glimmer of the glowing lake water dimmed into the darkness. I felt his energy sink into the water below us.

"Good thing for my aunt, man," he continued, his voice solemn and heavy. "She really saved me. I was in pretty bad shape after Pop passed."

I could feel the stride of our legs slow in unison, the churning vibration of the water falling into a rhythmic sync that seemed to ease my nerves and calm Gauge's self-conjured sorrow.

Without thought, I felt myself inch closer to him in the water.

"I'm sorry," I whispered, my kicking legs now centimeters from his.

"Nah, man," he replied, his voice lifting as the reflection of my moonlit face again filled the deep pools of his eyes. "It all happens as it's meant to, right?"

With that, he dropped below the surface and into the depths beyond. I felt his presence disappear from the sphere of liquid that surrounded me. Suddenly, the uncertainty of what lurked beneath us began to creep into my imagination. A laundry list of Everglades creatures began to scroll through the darkness of my mind like the opening sequence of Star Wars.

Without warning, Gauge rocketed out of the water, his shoulders sliding between my slow-kicking legs, forcing them into a sitting position. I felt him stumble and struggle to find his footing along the slimy bottom of the steeply descending lake bed. With a few wobbled hops, he pushed his full height from underneath the rippled liquid mirror and stood with the water now level with his knees. His hands gripped my thighs, firmly securing my position around his neck. I felt blood rushing into my lower extremities as my brain realized that my naked crotch was pressed flat against the backside of his head. I tried to distract myself, as I knew an erection was imminent.

Thankfully, before the vessels and veins of my body's most sensitive piece of dangling flesh could respond, Gauge threw me from his shoulders and into the deeper water behind us. In a semi-somersault, I fell below the surface with my eyes remaining open. As I sank into the blackness, my vision cleared, taking in the water-jumbled sight above me. There in the moonlight stood a fully nude Gauge, his entire body lit from the reflection of the water. The milky paleness of his bare skin glowed as bright as the moon, the only darkness the shadowed blur of his inked arm markings and the thickness of hair that surrounded his manhood.

I allowed the sight to imprint onto my brain like a tattoo needle pricking the flesh. I sank into the darkness, the all-consuming vision above me fading into the distance as though I were returning to life after a near-death experience. The seconds passed as an infinite eternity. Finally, with the ache of my oxygen-depleted lungs signaling their despair, I rose to the surface, my body breaking the water slow and delicately. Gauge was laughing as my vision cleared and my hearing returned from the echoed hollows of watered encapsulation. I moved toward him in my liquid haze, pushing his shoulder with all my strength. He stumbled, though I was sure it was half on purpose, allowing his body to drop backward into the lake. He catapulted back through the surface, his laughter more excited and joyous than before. Back and forth, we wrestled above the knee-deep water, the moon our stage light, the chirping crickets and groaning toads our cheering audience. I no longer focused on the fact that the man who had dominated my every thought and fantasy for the last three days was fully naked before me. Instead, I found myself completely engulfed in the playful yet competitive show of masculine bravado. The world faded around me, the deafening, ambient symphony of the surrounding Everglades circling and droning my senses, my vision and hearing becoming a fused sensation. I wasn't sure how long the tussled and splashed dance went on, but I experienced it in a very real and powerful sense of presence. Time was irrelevant, and thought was nonexistent. I simply lived in the moment, taking in its every detail as aware and focused as a cheetah observing the evening savannah.

Eventually, we began to tire, finding ourselves crouched in the lake water, our knees sinking into the soft skin of the sand. I listened in wonder as I heard myself begin to fill the sphere of sound that surrounded us with an onslaught of words. Stories and recollections of my childhood filled the air as thick and present as the palpable humidity that shrouded us like heavy garments.

My dreams and ambitions to become a famous actor detailed the storyline of my overflowing conversation. An embarrassing confession of losing my swim trunks at a church summer camp initiated Gauge's infectious laughter, the dazzled movement of the water projecting onto his dark eyes like tiny planets absorbing the brilliance of a nearby star. I told him of how I dreamed of standing beachside at the Pacific Ocean, feeling the colder waters of the westbound sea replacing the salt-tinge left by my lifelong existence near its eastern sister, the Atlantic. I even detailed the event at the bathhouse, my words somber and automatic. I didn't think before I spoke, I simply spoke. The truth and explicit accuracy of my story seemed to suffocate the world around us. I watched as tiny droplets of water peered over the rims of Gauge's eyes. I wasn't sure if they were a physical response to the emotion of my story or simply the remnants of the lake water or the dewing of the summer humidity. Either way, I completed my avalanche of self-exposure without agenda or hope of sympathy. Though I didn't quite understand why, there was an intense need in me to share with Gauge, even that which could be considered private and shameful. Sitting naked in a secluded lake eased my self-consciousness into a broken levee of soul revelation.

The mood was empty yet somehow comforting as we made our way back to the shore. Gauge didn't speak. I could tell he was now lost within the confines of his own mind, the sudden outpour of information swirling inside his head like a bayside waterspout. The intensity of the bathhouse story silenced his reactions. When he initiated the move back to the shore, I simply followed, somehow understanding his need for silence.

With our crumpled clothing again stretched across our bodies, we boarded the motorcycle and cruised into the Florida night. My heart beat easily as I rested my face against Gauge's back. At some point during the unaccounted hours of the evening, I felt closer to him. No friend or family member was ever able to get me to open up the way I had with Gauge, a man I had known no longer than a matter of days. Still, revealing myself to him was easy, both in soul and in flesh. It was as if I knew him already, his presence warm and familiar, as though we had shared many lifetimes together.

As we glided onto our street, Gauge cut the engine and clicked off the headlight. We sailed in a zephyr's silence as the momentum of the bike began to lull. Suddenly, Gauge squeezed the brake, halting the motorcycle in place.

"You don't deserve what happened to you," he stated, his voice shaking. "No one does."

I held my breath in silent suspense as he turned his head to face me.

"But especially not you."

This time, it was clear that the sudden arrival of water along the lower rims of his eyes was initiated by emotion. I felt my own vision begin to dampen as I realized the enormity of his reaction. It was obvious that he was deeply upset by what I had revealed to him. Regardless of the fact that we had only just met, it was transparent how much he cared for me.

Before I could reply, he restarted the bike and accelerated toward our neighboring houses.

In the shadows between the streetlights, I unfastened the helmet and handed it back to him. He nodded, his dark eyes reflecting the faint light of his aunt's living room window in the distance.

"Thanks for riding along with me, Dustin," he said gently over the idling grumble of the motorcycle's engine. "I had a good time, new friend."

Without waiting for a reply, he lifted his leg and twisted the throttle. I watched in the darkness as he rounded the side of his aunt's house and vanished out of sight.

My mind remained still as I moved along the side of my parents' house. Reentering the kitchen door, I slid through the dimly lit dining room and bounded up the stairs to my bedroom. Falling into bed, I slipped into an immediate, restful sleep.

Tonight, there were no dreams, no fantasies, for it was impossible for me to imagine anything more wonderful and surreal than what had just taken place.

***

UNSURPRISINGLY, MY MOTHER GAVE me hell the next morning. Sitting alongside my father at the breakfast table, a stack of overcooked pancakes before me, a streaming pile of what I assumed was oatmeal beside it, I kept my eyes fixated on the plate as my mother detailed the relentless, torturous state of worry that kept her up half the night. Apparently, it was just before I returned home when she finally drifted off to sleep, her stomach in knots, her imagination in shambles.

After apologizing and agreeing to never again leave the house without both notifying her and seeking her approval, I bounded back up the stairs to my room, slamming the door shut behind me.

I spent the next several hours flipping through old books and magazines, scribbling nonsense onto paper, and avoiding my mother at all costs, all the while peering obsessively out my window.

Just as the sun began to set and the streetlights flickered to life, I saw what I had been anticipating. There stood Gauge, the same denim jeans hugging his legs, a plain white T-shirt snuggly adorning his upper body. My pulse accelerated as I watched him take several long drags of a cigarette, the faint glow of the burning tobacco illuminating his face. He looked out over the street, his eyes roaming the distance of endless lawns and asphalt before taking a final pull of smoky air. Flicking the butt into the freshly cut grass, he turned toward the house. Just as he neared the side of the garage, he paused, gazing up at my window.

My heart stopped beating as our eyes locked.

He smiled, nodded, and then motioned for me to come out-side. I smiled back, an instant, instinctive reaction, and then stumbled backward into the middle of my room. I scrambled to change my clothing, realizing I was still wearing the same crumpled garments I had worn to the lake the night before.

Locating a pair of off-white tennis shorts and a maroon polo shirt, I tossed them on and excitedly rushed into the hallway. Deploying my perfected stairway stealth skills, I tiptoed downstairs and bounded out the front door.

Thankfully, my mother wasn't within seeing or hearing distance of my escape.

My heart drummed louder in my ears as I neared the side of Gauge's aunt's garage. He smiled as I approached him, my entire body reacting to the sight of his expression.

"Hey, man. Long time no see."

I could only smile as his booming voice draped over me like a thin nightshirt. Within seconds, I was standing face to face with him.

"I want you to meet my aunt," he said, a hint of excitement in his voice. "I've told her about you. She's anxious to say hello."

Before I could respond, Gauge began to lead the way along-side the garage and toward a side door. Without thought or hesitation, I followed, my steps falling in unison with his.

The garage smelled of rubber tires and gasoline. The tower of boxes I had seen through the living room window now dominated this area. I watched carefully as Gauge led the way through the labyrinth of cardboard and through a second doorway that led into the house.

Immediately, the smell of some sort of baked goods over-powered my nostrils.

"Aunt Mert!" Gauge called, his deep voice now light and boyish. "Aunt Mert, I've brought Dustin over."

A tiny woman appeared in the distance, her auburn curls piled carelessly above her head, a torn pair of bellbottom jeans covering her legs, a multicolored smock flowing with her movement.

"Well, hello, our dear new neighbor!" she exclaimed cheerfully as I neared her.

"Hi," I replied, my voice stumbling over my heartbeat.

"Gauge has told me all about you. I look forward to getting to know you myself."

Up close, I could see the age in Aunt Mert's eyes, her dimly lit baby blues sparkling in the faint light like the variety of crystals that hung loosely around her neck on a silver chain.

"Perhaps you could bring your parents by sometime," she continued, allowing her eyes to journey over every facet and feature of my face. "I always insist on getting to know my neighbors."

She paused, her eyes locking with mine.

"Especially kind and handsome neighbors such as yourself."

I felt myself blush, the heat from under my skin rivaling that of the nearby kitchen.

"Well," she stuck out her hand, some sort of powder substance covering one side, "it was a pleasure to meet you."

I clasped my hand with hers, the tender softness of her touch instantly easing my shy nerves.

"Thank you, Miss," I replied, allowing my eyes to stay connected with the glimmering glow of her gaze.

"Oh, now, call me Aunt Mert. I insist!"

I laughed with her, more out of politeness than actual humor. She winked at me as she spun on her heels and returned to the kitchen.

"This way," Gauge chimed in, gripping his fingers around my forearm. His touch was gentle yet sturdy. I followed his lead through the shadows of the faintly lit house until we came to a half-opened door.

Gauge dropped my arm and ventured into the blackness. Fumbling blindly, he murmured to himself as he struggled to locate a lamp switch.

Finally finding it, the darkness retreated, leaving behind an open space of complete disarray.

Stacks of cardboard boxes aligned the walls, piles of clothing and books littered the blue shag carpet. My eyes spied a stack of *Playboy* magazines just next to the disheveled bed.

"Sorry for the mess, man. Unpacking is a bitch."

He dropped onto the bed, his carefully combed hair spreading over his white pillow like dark grass blades over a fresh snow.

He patted the open space beside him, signaling for me to join.

"Take a look at this," he stated, lifting himself into a sitting position. He pulled a large leather book from the cluttered nightstand that hosted the lamp. "This was my pop's."

He peeled open the book, a photo album, the plastic sleeves squeaking as he pulled them apart.

My eyes toured a collage of yellowed photographs. A handsome man, resembling what I imagined Gauge to look like in a few decades, filled the space of each square paper, the photos a mix of prints and Polaroids.

"Here's the Indian," he said proudly, his finger tapping a small print in the lower-right corner of the book.

The handsome man sat on top of the bike, which was far cleaner and newer-looking, the same crooked smile I had seen on Gauge etched across his face.

"Dad loved that bike, man," he continued, his voice drifting with his eyes. "I know he'd be proud that I've been rebuilding the engine again."

I watched quietly as he stared at the photograph.

"Still have a ways to go with it."

Several seconds passed before he spoke again.

"We will get it there, though. Won't we?"

His eyes met mine, a tinge of wetness twinkling between each set of lashes. I swallowed in nervousness as the mood of the room suddenly became heavy and emotional.

"Hey," Gauge broke the silence. "Check out these puppies. They were my dad's too."

He leaned over the side of the bed, lifting the pile of *Playboys* into his arms.

An endless spread of magazines slid over the photo album as he dropped them from his grip.

"Dad loved the ladies," he laughed, flipping the pages of one of the issues.

"I mean, come on," he continued, holding up one of the centerfolds. "Who doesn't love this?"

I blushed as he dropped the open spread onto my lap.

"Look at those tits, man. Just beautiful."

My eyes absorbed the site of a busty female, her dark hair shining in the sun, her eyes heavy with blue makeup.

I looked away as my brain began to take in the site of her nipples and pubic hair.

"What about you, Dustin?" he questioned, his eyes awaiting mine. "You have a girl?"

I nearly choked. I didn't know how to respond. The sudden personal question not only caught me off guard but also alarmed my nerves and stoked my discomfort. The mixture of the naked female and Gauge's pressing gaze was both cringeworthy and intimidating.

"Hey, man," he continued after I failed to respond. "It's cool. There is plenty of time to make it with the ladies."

He closed the *Playboy*, tossing it to the floor before scooping up the others and dropping them to the same fate. Carefully, he closed the photo album, the tender care he displayed revealing the importance of the leather-bound book over that of the endless stack of magazines.

"Do you have a girl?" I managed to ask, my voice surprisingly calm and firm.

He looked up at me, a slight pause before a smile broke across his lips.

"I did," he answered, his eyes drifting to the corner of the room. "Her name was Rebecca. Cute girl, man. I really dug her. She broke up with me when I told her I was moving. She said she couldn't deal with the long-distance thing."

"Where did you move from?" I asked, an unfamiliar tinge icing over my words, a knife-like prick dancing across my gut as he spoke of the girl.

"Milwaukee," he replied, a slight laughter accenting his words. "Place is cold and boring as shit, man. Aunt Mert got a good transfer here, so we headed down."

Again, his words drifted into his silent thoughts.

"I came along. With Pop gone, there really wasn't much for me to do up there."

He let out a breathy chuckle.

"Well, besides Rebecca of course."

He burst into laughter, his hair grazing the tops of his eyebrows like feathers from a raven's wing.

I sat in silence before forcing a returned laugh, reeling from the flashing images of Gauge and some girl that my imagination forced across the vision of my mind.

"Down here, man," he continued, his voice calming from his laughter, "the girls are beautiful. I love hanging out at the beach just to check out all the women in bikinis."

He waited for my eyes to reconnect with his.

"Jerking material for days, you know what I mean?"

I humored him with a returned laugh as I followed my sinking heart as it came to terms with the reality that Gauge was attracted to the opposite sex. A bitter chill clouded over my one-sided fantasies like an unexpected blizzard rolling across the Canadian countryside. I began to plan my excuse to leave, when Gauge grabbed my arm.

"Come on," he said with excitement, pulling me from the bed and into the darkened hallway.

I followed blindly, the gentle security of his hand around my wrist my only guiding point. Within seconds, we were back in the garage, the unmistakable thickness of heat and humidity absorbing our bodies like an invisible quicksand.

My eyes adjusted to the dim lighting as Gauge shuffled through the massive array of cardboard boxes. I located a stack of yellowed newspapers to sit on as I waited for him to find whatever it was he was searching for.

"Here we go," he announced as he pulled a pile of books and papers from one of the endless boxes. "I was scared for a minute that maybe these didn't make it down here with us."

He moved toward me, crouching down to match my seated height.

"I've got the entire thing mapped," he said, opening a disheveled notebook, pamphlets and map clippings spilling from its pages and onto my lap.

"What is all of this?" I asked, allowing my fingers to shuffle through the overflow as it continued to fall across my legs.

"You said you wanted to be an actor, right?" Gauge asked, our eyes meeting.

"Yeah," I replied cautiously, unsure as to where he was going with this. I was accustomed to my mother mocking me whenever the topic of my dreams to become an actor arose. To her, such ambitions were merely far-fetched delusions that distracted me from a more realistic and tangible career path. I suddenly regretted even mentioning the topic to Gauge.

"Well, if you wanna be a movie star, you gotta go to Hollywood, right?"

He moved his hands to reveal a worn and tattered map of the United States. Streaked across it, like a wild vine stretching the side of an old church wall, was a blood-red marker stripe that highlighted the highways and interstates that would lead to the west coast from the east.

"This is my second edition," Gauge continued, carefully managing the fragile paper in his hands. "The original was from Milwaukee to LA, but I started over when I knew I was gonna be heading down here."

He lifted his gaze to mine.

"I've always dreamed of going to the West Coast."

He flipped through the notebook, locating several brochures on California.

"See," he declared, as though he needed to provide evidence for his statement.

"Like you, I've always wanted to swim in the Pacific."

He shuffled the pages of the brochure until he came to a full-page photograph of several surfers riding the crest of a mammoth wave.

"I mean, the Atlantic is beautiful and all, but dude, you can't do this down here."

His eyes sparkled with pure enthusiasm as he moved his fingers over the image. I could tell that in his mind, he was there, the power of the water surging beneath him, the blast of the California sun heating his pores with a crisp dryness that lacked the suffocating humidity that plagued the Florida air. I felt myself begin to crack a smile as I took in his excitement. His passion was palpable, his childlike dreaminess inspiring and addictive.

"We should road-trip out there," he said, his eyes still scanning the photograph. "Think about that ride, man. Crossing the country. We'd see everything."

My heart fluttered as I listened to him include me in his plans. The feeling of disappointment regarding the reality of our connection began to fade as I realized I would rather continue pursuing a genuine friendship with this kindhearted man than impose any sort of imagined or fantasy-driven illusion. Despite any uncontrolled, deep-rooted fantasies and desires I held for Gauge, my wish to just remain near him, at whatever capacity, was enough to sustain me.

"Then when we got there we could check out some auditions for you to do or something."

I could only stare at him, shocked and amazed at not only his interest in me and my dreams, but also his belief and support in them. I had never experienced anything like this before.

"Would you like that?"

Again, I could only stare, several seconds passing before I could forcefully muster a verbal response.

"Yeah, sure," I warbled, my voice awkward and uncertain. "I think that would be great."

"Cool," Gauge smiled, closing the notebook over the sea of spilled contents. "Maybe after I save up some dough we could try and head out there."

I nodded.

"Yeah," my voice cracking over my confusion. "Yeah, that sounds good."

Here was a person I had only known a matter of days, yet he not only encouraged my lofty goals and ambitions, but he also offered to be a part of them, assisting me across the country after just one rambling conversation while crouched naked in a lake.

"Let's do it then," he declared while standing to his feet. "I'm gonna keep these out so that we stay aware of the plan."

I met his eyes, the gleam of California dreams still turning inside his pupils like the moon's steadfast rotation around the Earth.

"Come on," Gauge motioned with his arm. "Let's go see what Aunt Mert baked up."

I followed him, again allowing my feet to simply move in the direction of his voice.

I listened as Gauge continued a laugh-heavy, one-sided conversation about the colorful characters he knew in Milwaukee. In the shadows of the dark house, I smiled, content to be alongside this man, wading in the warm pool of his words as calm and peaceful as a swan gliding over a summer pond. In the distance, the inviting aroma of his aunt's freshly baked delights beckoned us toward the kitchen like two worker bees obeying the pheromone release of the queen.

I spent the next two hours fully immersed and engaged with my new neighbors, absorbing their stories and laughter like the cracked, barren desert floor after the first rainstorm of a three-year drought. Time slipped by without notice, the comfort and joy of the shared company filling the space around us as warm and inviting as the appetizing smell of Aunt Mert's baking.

The house was still and quiet when I finally returned home. I was surprised that my mother was not around someplace waiting for me. I glided up the stairs and slipped into my bed unnoticed. A smile stretched across my face as I faded into the darkness, my heart beating softly, my mind calm and at ease.

***

I SPENT EVERY DAY with Gauge. The remainder of the summer consisted of return trips to the lake; long, lazy days at Hollywood Beach; or even countless hours spent at our houses, playing cards, watching movies, or just talking in the backyard.

My mother was suspicious of Gauge. I could tell by the way she looked at him. She was polite enough, but her demeanor and cautious line of questioning each time he was around was enough for me to realize her uncertainty about him. Gauge was always respectful and kind to her, so I was never quite sure what caused her subtle, but obvious to me, disdain. It was as if she knew something about him but wasn't quite sure how to explain it. If she could, she most certainly would have said something to me by now.

I didn't care, though. I was happy just being with Gauge. It didn't matter what we did or where we went. As long as we were together, I was content. The days rolled past us like train cars on an endless track, the miles yet to travel blurred and faded by the heated wave of distance.

Our daily routine became so consistent that I could practically predict the next day's events without even suggesting or questioning a thing.

We would meet sometime in the early afternoon and partake in whatever activity far into the night. This had become so methodical and expected that my mother would no longer ask who I was with or where I was going. Though she was not fully approving of my company, she allowed me the freedom, and only harped on me for neglecting chores or leaving dirty clothes on the bathroom floor.

Then, one day in late August, everything changed.

The day began like any other, the summer sun scorching the Florida sky like a flame dancing over a pool of gasoline. The stale summer air sat heavy over the humid landscape like a giant, sticky, thick Jell-O mold. The sound of the blue jays and black grackles echoed over the treetops like a summer song. The droning buzz of the nearby powerlines sizzled over the rooftops, replacing the distant sound of the voices of children, who had recently returned to school.

I met Gauge in front of Aunt Mert's garage. With a giant smile locked across his handsome face, he motioned for me to follow him, putting a finger to his lips to signal my silence. Obeying his lead, I shuffled behind him toward the back of the house, Aunt Mert's giant orange trees commanding their presence with an overflow of oranges, both ripe and rotten. The smell of the citrus fruit seared my nostrils, the sharp, pungent aroma invading every centimeter of my sinus cavity.

I stood in place as Gauge crept into the corner near the shed. Removing a debris pile that consisted of rusted tools and yellowed newspapers, he retrieved a large, clear bottle filled to the brim with some sort of brown liquid. With the excited smile still emblazoned across his lips, he bounced back to me, tucking his secret treasure in his arm as if to conceal its obvious identity.

"Jack fucking Daniel's," he announced excitedly as he lifted the bottle near my face. "A brand-new bottle, my friend."

One would have thought Gauge had stumbled upon the Holy Grail by the amount of excitement in his voice. Aside from when he spoke of riding the Indian to the West Coast, I had yet to witness Gauge so stimulated. It was as if locating the bottle of Jack had earned him some unseen fortune. I certainly was not as impressed by the unexpected discovery of the liquor as he was.

"Let's get fucked up!" he declared to the entire backyard.

"Gauge, wait. I don't think it's a good idea to—"

Gauge stuck the now open bottle rim to my lips, lifting it high so that the warm contents would slip into my mouth. A stinging rush of alcohol washed over my tongue and down my throat. I began to choke and gasp for air as the whiskey singed its way down my trachea and into my stomach.

"Aw, come on now, man. Don't pussy out on me. I know this ain't your first time taking a swig of ol' Jack!"

Hot tears began to stream down my cheeks as I struggled to catch my breath. A twisting vine of laughter and anger began to rise within my core as I slowly regained my composure.

"You asshole!" I yelled, punching him in the chest. "That shit burned like hell!"

I couldn't help but smile as I watched Gauge's face pinch into a fit of laughter, his joyous, deep voice booming around me like thunder over the open sea. Any tinge of anger I felt quickly faded into the fog of my infatuation. As much as I had been resisting, I had fallen in love with Gauge, my heart willing and open, yet fully aware of the one-sided desire.

"Man, I wish you could have seen your face," he continued, his words broken by his steady laughter. "You woulda thought I shoved battery acid down your hatch."

I laughed with him, the forgiveness brought on by love quick and instant, yet strong and definite.

"Come on," he said, nodding his head toward the back side of the shed.

I followed him to the pile of cinderblocks that aligned the rusted aluminum wall, and sat beside him. I watched in amusement as he began to chug the whiskey.

"Where did you even find this?" I asked, suddenly concerned that he was downing a substance that had perhaps been lying dormant in the yard for who knows how long.

"It was my pop's" he answered, keeping his eyes trained on the weed-covered chain link fence that stood just feet before us. "I found it in one of the boxes of his things."

We sat in silence as he continued to drink. The innocent partaking of something forbidden had suddenly become a somber yet spiritual experience. It was as if consuming the bottle of Jack Daniel's was somehow connecting Gauge to his deceased father. I no longer felt the need to stop him. I simply remained still and observed as he continued with haste.

"Here," he said several minutes later, slowly moving the now half-empty bottle toward me.

Not wanting to disappoint him, I accepted the large glass container and lifted it to my lips. Filling my mouth with another giant gulp, I held my breath as the burning liquid permeated my upper body like a poison. As much as I dreaded the awful taste of its contents, the chance to share the bottle's rim provided me the opportunity to exchange saliva with Gauge. It was the closest I would ever get to kissing him. Or so I thought.

Just as I was lowering the cylindrical neck from my whiskey-soaked mouth, Gauge knocked the heavy canister from my hand, the sound of the remaining liquid as it glugged across the soft dirt proceeding that of the muffled thud of the bottle.

I lost all sense of time and space as Gauge pressed his wet lips onto mine. I didn't move, I didn't breathe, I wasn't even sure if my heart was still beating. I merely remained still, the overwhelming scent of Jack Daniel's consuming the shared air between us.

His face was shaking, his body trembling. I wrapped my arms around him, choking back a sudden sob as he lifted both hands to cup my face. I opened my eyes to see the reflection of my expression staring back at me in the darkness of his gentle gaze, my brimming tears evident even in the shadowed closeness of our faces. I watched as my reflection fell from the black hole of his eyes and down the pinkness of his cheeks. The sob escaped me as he again pressed his lips to mine, our skin so close that the water of our eyes began to mingle like the confluence of two rivers.

In the distance, a lawn mower fired to life and a dog barked at the sound. Reality found us, and a space fell between our lips. I could only stare at Gauge, too amazed and shocked to move or speak. I watched as he wiped the liquor and saliva from his mouth and stood in place. Brushing some dirt from his jeans, he moved to the chain-link fence and leaned against it, his face turned to the neighboring yard.

I stood and moved to stand beside him, when he stopped me.

"Go home, Dustin," he said softly, keeping his face straight ahead.

I thought to speak, but no words found me. I nodded, knowing full well that Gauge could not see me, and turned to leave. All of me wanted him to stop me as I crossed the distance between the shed and the side of the house. I didn't turn back or even glance over my shoulder. I simply kept moving forward, a knot around my heart that wrapped tighter with each step.

A flood of tears greeted me as I rounded the side of Aunt Mert's house and bounded across her lawn toward home. Once inside, I paused at the front door, attempting to regain my emotional composure. Slowly, I ascended the stairs and turned the corner toward my bedroom. It was then that I nearly collided with my mother.

"What's the matter?" she queried, squinting her eyes in the dim hallway light. "Have you been crying?"

"No," I replied without hesitation. "Someone is cutting their lawn and the dust has my allergies all flared up."

She continued to stare at me, her eyes twinkling with the certainty of disbelief.

"You need to clean your room," she finally spoke, her face still transparent with her knowledge of the truth. "And I mean all of it. Vacuuming, dusting. Don't just throw stuff under the bed and think I won't see it."

I rolled my eyes as I passed her.

"And don't roll your eyes at me, young man. I will not be disrespected."

I turned to face her, my skin still damp with tears.

"I will have you know that I am being more than patient with you right now," she continued, adjusting the clarity and firmness of her voice. I could tell she had been waiting to have this conversation with me.

"Your father and I are not too happy with all the time you have been spending with that neighbor boy."

She steadied her eyes on mine, her anticipation of my response, verbal or otherwise, as intense and powerful as a lioness crouching just feet from an infant gazelle.

"There is something about him we are not too keen on," she stated, her face stern, her eyes unmoving. "I am not sure what it is, but it's enough for us to say that we think you would be better off just staying away from him."

I could only stare, the broken levee of my emotions too uncontrolled and flooded for me to begin processing her words.

"Plus, I think it is high time you figure out what you are going to do."

She waited for my reply but continued to speak when I failed to do so in the time allotted by her patience.

"You need to either get your butt back in school or get a job. But you are certainly not going to hang around here all the time doing God knows what with that boy."

She threw her head in the direction of Aunt Mert's, her face now crinkled and aged under the unrelenting weight of her disapproval.

"He is probably on drugs or something. He looks like he hasn't bathed in weeks, and I would bet he didn't even complete high school."

I continued to stare, my pulse now racing, the flooded valley of my emotions now boiling with the rising rage of anger.

"He's a loser, Dustin. You are so much better than someone like him. Don't let him drag you down. You need some better friends. I think you should get out and go to—"

"I love him!" I shouted, my voice so loud and unexpected that it startled even me.

I watched as my mother's face melted from selfish anger to sudden horror.

"What?" she murmured, her expression alarmed, her hands reaching for the security of the hallway wall.

With the levee already broken, I found strength and courage in the raging waters of truth that now rushed beyond the normally secured and steadfast concrete emotional embankment.

Without warning or thought, without a plan or even an inspiration, I flooded my mother with a truth that I myself had been too afraid to fully accept and embrace, much less speak out loud. Still, the words fell from my mouth as solid and honest as an elephant's sturdy footsteps across an African plain.

"That's right, Mom," I bellowed into the space between us. "I'm gay!"

I watched as my mother nearly fell over, her head bobbing slightly to the side as her feet shuffled beneath her. Instinctively, I moved toward her.

"Mom," I called as I approached her. "Mom, look at me."

The stinging rush of pain triggered by the open impact of her hand to my face electrified the nerves of my head like a lightning bolt. I swallowed hard, the nervous dryness of my throat relieved by the sliding moisture as it passed. I took in a breath before turning to fully face her again.

"No," she growled through tightly clenched teeth. "No son of mine is gay. No!"

Again, she raised her hand to slap me, but this time I moved to the opposite side of the hall, leaving the power of her arm to strike a family portrait that adorned the wall that had stood beside me.

"No!" she screamed again, this time the presence of fearful tears clogging the projection of her voice.

"Yes, Mom," I continued, my own voice wobbled and shaken. "It's true. I have always known it. It just took me a while to finally understand it."

She lifted her eyes and glared at me, the shadows of a million confirmed suspicions escaping her skull like bats fleeing a dynamited cavern.

"It isn't true!" she yelled back, her eyes bulged and watered. "You know it isn't true."

"But it is, Mom! It is!"

I felt myself fall back against the wall, my spine slowly inching my body to the floor.

"Is that why you were at the bathhouse?"

I looked up as she fell from her unstable stance to a crouched squat. We were now eye to eye, perched like vultures over a rotting carcass.

"Were you really raped or was it just sex?"

I closed my eyes as she crawled toward me, her hands and feet scraping the wooden hallway floor like a crab scurrying across a dry boat dock.

"Is that what really happened?" she asked as she closed in on me, her rage and disappointment now staining her face, her sky-blue mascara running with her tears.

"Answer me!" she shouted, her face only inches from mine.

"No!" I screamed back. "No, I was attacked. I went there on purpose, but I was attacked...raped!"

I opened my eyes just as my mother dropped her weight onto my chest.

"No, no, no," she sobbed into my shirt, the smell of her faint perfume seeping through the air and into my nose.

"I'm sorry, Mom," I whispered, placing my hands on her trembling shoulders. "I don't mean to hurt you. This is just the truth. This is who I am."

"No," she spoke with confidence as she raised her head. "This is not who you are. This is what people have told you. This isn't you. It was probably that boy. He put all this into your head. I should have known he was some sort of pervert. He—"

"Stop!" I cried, pushing her from my chest and to the open area of the hallway. "It's nothing like that. He has nothing to do with this."

"The hell he doesn't," she scoffed, lifting herself from the floor.

"You listen here, boy," she seethed, her voice now dark and hollow. "No child of mine will ever live under my roof while partaking in some disgusting lifestyle of unnatural...whatever."

She paused, ensuring that my eyes were locked on hers. "It's sinful and it's revolting."

She directed her words at me, as fiery and dangerous as a burning arrow. She was certain to strike the softness of my emotional belly with her angered intent.

"We are going to get you to someone," she announced breathlessly as she moved toward me. "There are people you can talk to about this. People who can help you sort out this confusion you are feeling."

She lifted her hand to cover my mouth before I could respond.

"But most of all," she stated in a bone-chilling tone, "your father must never know about this."

She moved her eyes into the dim light.

"He will disown you."

With that, she slowly spun on her heels and disappeared toward the stairway. My heart beat in unison with the creaking boards as she neared the first floor. I allowed myself to fall back against my closed bedroom door, the enormity of what had just occurred replaying through my mind like a flapping bedsheet left out in a Kansas rainstorm. It was several minutes before I could muster the energy to turn the knob and move into the room.

Closing the door behind me, I fell to my knees, my sobbing tearless, my breathing broken and exhausted.

Just as the sun set beyond the rooftops, I cried myself to sleep, the haunting voices of a dismissive Gauge and a raging, unaccepting mother pressed upon my heart like some Shroud of Turin that neither time nor tundra could erase.

***

I HARDLY LEFT MY room for the next three days. During the few, brief encounters I had with my mother, she barely glanced at me, much less spoke. In the middle of the second night, I heard her sobbing in the downstairs guest bathroom as I made my way from the kitchen. She was there to avoid disturbing my father, and I imagined that her tears were over me.

I obsessively glanced out my bedroom window, praying to catch a glimpse of Gauge. I never did. For three days straight, not a shred of evidence of his existence could be found. I would see Aunt Mert's giant silver Cadillac backing down the driveway, returning eight or so hours later like clockwork. Still, no Gauge.

As the sun was setting on the third day, I finally heard his voice. Cracking my window, I pressed my ear into the wind, allowing the small bones to sense the direction of the voice. It took me several minutes to figure out that it was coming from the backyard. It sounded like he was speaking to Aunt Mert, her high Midwestern drawl peppering the conversation from time to time, accenting the powerful bass of Gauge's baritone like a wind chime.

On the fourth day, I went outside. Standing in the drive-way, I watched as some neighborhood children made their way from the school bus stop. Their carefree chatter and laughter swirled around me like a soft breeze in the stale, humid air, lifting some of the heaviness of my burdened and troubled mind.

I envied their innocence. Life had yet to penetrate their silk-like childhoods. If only I could recapture my own trouble-free existence. If only I could go back. Back before the bathhouse. Back before meeting Gauge. Back before breaking my mother's heart.

"Hey."

I turned to see Gauge standing beside me, his shirt off, his worn blue jeans creased and wrinkled from what appeared to be extended wear.

"Hey," I replied, my voice creaking to life for the first time in days.

"Sorry about the other day, man," he said, his eyes connected to mine. "I shouldn't have messed with that Jack Daniel's."

He brushed his hands over the sides of his jeans.

"I shouldn't have done what I did."

I watched as he lifted his hands to rub his face, some sort of greasy residue sliding across his skin like a tribal war paint.

"It's..." my voice broke into silence. "It's okay."

"Cool," he responded, his nervousness giving way to relief. "Wanna see what I've been doing to the Indian?"

I stared at him, my eyes unable to blink, my brain unable to think.

"Come on," he grabbed my hand and pulled me toward the garage.

Before I could react, we were inside Aunt Mert's open garage, the 1949 Indian in pieces all over the solid concrete floor.

"I am completely refurbishing the carburetor," he announced, squatting to adjust some of the chrome pieces.

"When I'm done, this baby will be ready for the wide-open road."

He stood to face me.

"We could make it out to LA."

I closed my eyes, the silly dream-talk now a faded memory, yet present annoyance.

"Look, Gauge," I started, forcing my voice into a stable and focused key.

"Well, look who it is!" a high-pitched female voice broke into the space around us. "I haven't seen you in days! For a while there, I thought you two were conjoined twins or something."

I turned to see Aunt Mert, a tray of blueberry muffins perched upon her flattened right hand.

"I figured my Gauge was working up an appetite out here, so I tossed in some of these muffins I baked up for work this morning."

She moved the tray between Gauge and me.

"Please, boys, eat up. Heaven knows I don't need to eat any more of these!"

She laughed, her girlish giggle cleansing the air of the emotionally heavy fog that had only recently set in.

"Thanks, Aunt Mert," Gauge chimed in, lifting one of the oversized muffins from the tray. "These babies are my favorite."

Aunt Mert and I watched as he peeled down the paper wrapper and shoved the entire morsel into his mouth.

"Well, dear me!" Aunt Mert responded in a sing-song voice. "It isn't like someone is going to take it from you, dear. You know you can take more than one bite."

Gauge smiled, his cheeks stuffed to capacity, bobbing left and right as he struggled to consume the muffin.

"So, how've you been, Dustin?" Aunt Mert questioned, her lilac scent wafting through the garage like an invisible purple scarf.

"Doing fine," I lied, my eyes glazed with the truth of pain.

"I see," Aunt Mert replied, her eyes confirming that she didn't believe me. "Well, I'll leave you boys to it then."

I watched as the tiny red-haired woman glided back into the house, the smell of her muffins and perfume swirling behind her like a majestic cape.

I turned back to Gauge, who was still attempting to swallow the contents of his mouth.

"Goddamn, Gauge. You're gonna kill yourself eating that way."

He chuckled, the sound of his laughter absorbed by the mass of sugary dough churning inside his jaws.

"Okay, so listen," I started again, this time my words calm and stable. "Things are not good for me at home right now."

Gauge's face morphed from playful to serious.

"I said some things to my mom that I guess I shouldn't have."

I dropped my eyes to the floor, the lack of confidence and uncertainty that consumed me now as plain as the flesh that surrounded my bones.

"I think it's best that I don't hang out with you so much right now."

With an audible gulp, Gauge swallowed the mashed muffin and focused on catching his breath.

"What do you mean?" he questioned, his voice bursting with concern. "What did you say to her?"

"I don't want to talk about it," I fired back, my anger launched from the surface of the deep pool of shame and regret that filled my being.

"Okay," Gauge replied softly, placing a hand on my shoulder. "You know I'm here for you, Dustin," he spoke gently, his booming voice now fragile and sincere.

He placed his index finger under my chin, lifting my face to his.

"Always."

His breath was heavy with the sweetness of the blueberry muffin. My heart beat faster as I realized how close I was to him, the tenderness of his ruby lips glistening from the caress of his tongue. The burning desire I had buried three days prior now reignited beneath the flimsy covering of my contrived mental block like an inferno below a forest canopy.

"Thank you," I whispered, a tear escaping my left eye. I wiped it away before Gauge could notice, too afraid to allow this encounter to become any heavier than it already was. "That means a lot."

"This is about the fourth time I've rebuilt this carburetor," he announced after a few seconds of silence, stepping aside to allow the deconstructed motorcycle engine take the focus. "I've built and rebuilt this engine so many times I am beginning to wonder if it is even worth the trouble."

He brought his eyes back to mine.

"Junkyard parts, ya know. I guess you get what you pay for."

He laughed, his crooked smile revealing a rogue blueberry bit smashed and stuck between two of his front teeth.

"Blueberry stuck in your teeth," I stated, pointing to it. I watched as he leaned toward the Indian's left chrome mirror, sliding the baked fruit away in a unified movement of fingertip and tongue.

"Well, I need to get back home, Gauge," I said, moving to the open garage door. A rare, slightly crisp breeze greeted me as I edged the covering of the roof.

"Wait," Gauge boomed, his voice halting my movement.

I didn't look at him as he neared me, the heat from his skin overpowering the remaining hint of the elusive breeze.

"I want you to know that I didn't mean to upset you," his voice quivered, his struggling breath lost to the final sweep of the escaping wind. "That is the last thing I would ever want to do."

I could feel him staring at me, the presence of discomfort and guilt practically another being standing in the small space between us.

"I know, Gauge," I said, lifting my eyes to his. "You've already apologized, and I've already told you it was okay."

I rested my left hand lightly on his shoulder, waiting for his gaze to steady over mine.

"We are past this."

He nodded, relief melting from him like the droplets of salt-laced dew that covered his furrowed brow.

"I'll see you later," I concluded calmly, the weight of my hidden emotions now so cumbersome it was as if I were wading in a mud pit. Still, I managed a confident stride down the driveway and onto the sidewalk that led back to my parent's house.

I didn't stop once I was inside. I slowly ascended the stairs, rounded the corner to my bedroom, and slipped inside the door. Falling face first into my pillow, I started to drift away, the churning of emotions silently slipping through my body like the sluggish sands of an hourglass. I was just starting to doze when I heard my bedroom door open, the pressure of the hallway air filling my room like a fast-rolling fog.

I lifted my face and saw my mother, her image slowly clearing into view beneath the haze of impending sleep and waterless tears. She was in her nightgown, an enormous glass of red wine in one hand, her rarely touched Bible in the other.

She took a giant chug of wine before fully entering the room, closing the door quietly behind her.

"Mom?" I whispered, quickly lifting my body into a sitting position. My heart began to race at the surprise of not only her presence, but also the unusual appearance of her nightgown at such an early hour, and the holy book, which she only seemed to touch on Easter Sunday or take to funerals.

"Shh," she hissed at me, stumbling a bit as she made her way to the bed. "I don't want your father to hear me in here."

"Okay?" I answered inquisitively, darting my eyes toward the door as if expecting my father to appear at the mention of his name.

"Mom, what's going—"

"Shh!" she commanded, shoving her wine-stained finger over my lips.

She sat beside me, bending slowly to set the wine glass on the floor. She groaned a bit as she lifted her body back into place, turning to me with a clouded, tear-stained face.

"I've been doing a lot of thinking," she whispered, her voice raw in a cocktail of fermented grapes and emotion.

I watched as she fumbled the pages of her Bible, a coupon for hair removal cream falling to the floor as she located a space in the massive tome.

"This," she pointed, shoving the neatly crisp pages onto my lap. "Read what I've highlighted."

My eyes struggled to focus in the dim lighting of the room. Slowly, the brightly highlighted blurb came into view, a condemning passage from Leviticus, ripe with the judgment of abomination.

I sighed, pushing the Bible from my lap, allowing it to fall into the small space between us.

"Did you read it, Dustin? Did you see what God says about man lying with another man?"

She fumbled for the Bible, lifting it and plopping it back onto my lap.

"It's an abomination!" she hissed through clenched teeth, her breath as vile as her twisted expression.

"An abomination," she whispered again, this time her voice breaking to the flooding of tears that poured down her face.

"Mom," I cooed softly, placing my hands over hers. "Mom, please. Please don't do this to yourself."

She kept her head down, her shoulders trembling under the weight of her sobbing. I moved to embrace her, when she rose like a king cobra to meet my line of sight.

"Don't you patronize me, boy," she seethed, her face gleaming in the soft light of the small lamp that adorned my dresser. "I am trying to help you."

She allowed her head to fall back to her chest, her tear-heavy breathing shallow and labored. I remained still, too afraid to speak or move. Her emotions made her unsteady while the alcohol rendered her unpredictable. I feared a repeat of our hallway encounter.

"I love you, son," she sputtered, saliva mixing with the tears that had slipped over her upper lip. "I want the best for you. You know that."

She lifted her eyes to mine, my reflection lost in the pool of fear and sadness that overwhelmed her face.

"Yes," I swallowed, choking back my own rising emotion. "I know that, Mom, but you have to understand, this is not something I've chosen. It is just what I feel."

I lowered my hands back over hers, gripping them onto her shaking, tightly balled fists.

"It's just natural."

"No!" she screamed, knocking my hands from hers, apparently forgetting or uncaring as to the volume of her voice.

"There is nothing natural about this!" she shouted into my face, droplets of wine and tears splattering onto my skin like a warm ocean spray over a dry sea wall.

"You are just young. Confused."

She lifted herself from the bed, turning to reach for her Bible.

"I want you to speak with the pastor," she commanded, her words now controlled and direct.

"I have already made the arrangements. You meet with him tomorrow afternoon."

She squatted to the floor, crouching before her glass of wine like a hobbit locating some mystical brew.

"Mom, I...no."

My words stumbled from my lips as if coated with hot lead.

"I can't, Mom. No."

She rose to her feet and inched toward me, her eyes glaring down in a tornadic spin of terror-driven control.

"As long as you live in this house," she began, her voice cold and suddenly emotionless, "you will do as you are told."

She turned to leave. I jumped to my feet, anger bursting from beneath my breastbone and up the passageway of my throat. I hurled my words at the back of her head as if warding off a prowling predator.

"It's only love!" I shouted, my voice strong but breaking under the enormity of my funneled hurt. "What is so wrong with being in love?"

She turned and stared at me, her expression frozen, yet revealing a tinge of what appeared to be curiosity.

"It's not love," she whispered, lifting her hand to cup my cheek. "It's only confusion. You are too young to know what real love is anyway. You are just finding your way, and sometimes we need guidance in doing that."

She cradled her Bible against her breast, her free hand still clasped against my skin.

"We will get this sorted out."

She turned again, squatting back down to her wine glass,

this time wrapping her fingers around it like a deep-sea squid collecting its meal.

"I promise, my love," she said softly as she lifted to her full height, her knees creaking and popping at the motion. "You will thank me for this in time."

"Mom—"

My words were interrupted by the sudden appearance of my father, his face weighted with concern, his eyes darting between my mother and me as if absorbing the sight of two restless ghosts.

"Everything all right in here?" he questioned gently, his gaze finally settling onto my mother.

"You okay, dear?" he asked, nervously moving into the room from behind the door. "You look like you've been crying."

She halted him with her words as he neared her.

"I'm fine, Nathan," she scolded. "Your son and I were only talking."

My father looked at me inquisitively, his soft eyes labored with concern.

I forced a small smile at him before allowing my eyes to trail the room to the closet. I was afraid any extended eye contact would lead to more questioning.

"I heard shouting," he continued, turning his attention back to my mother. "Are you sure everything is okay?"

"Yes, Nathan," my mother snapped. "Just go back downstairs. I am coming down in a minute."

"Okay," he concluded after a moment of confused silence.

I didn't raise my eyes as I felt him take one last look at me before obeying the order to leave. It was at least a minute before my mother spun on her heels to face me.

"Tomorrow," she stated flatly, waiting for my gaze to meet hers. "I will drive you."

She peered over her shoulder at the closed bedroom door.

"Say nothing about any of this to your father," she commanded, returning her head and centering her face before my eyes. "He can't handle something like this."

Slowly, she pivoted to face the door but didn't move forward.

"I love you, Dustin," she said in a shaken whisper without looking back. "I can't lose you."

Before I could question what she meant, she darted into the hallway and disappeared into the darkness.

Stunned, shocked, and completely overwhelmed, I collapsed onto my bed and drifted off into an immediate yet restless sleep.

***

THREE WEEKS LATER, I sat alone on the front step, the quiet of the neighborhood a stark contrast to the relentless noise inside my head. The meeting with the pastor had gone relatively well. He was a kind man, gentle eyes, who was more interested in recanting tales of his own youth than resolving my supposed "problem." In between seemingly exaggerated stories of his athletic prowess, he rattled off a few Bible verses and then prayed for God's wisdom to guide my path. Afterward, he said a few words to my mother, who had waited impatiently just outside his office. Throughout the entire hour-long session, I was distracted by her silhouette as she paced back and forth behind the frosted glass of the office door.

Whatever the pastor said to her seemed to relieve her fear, as she hadn't mentioned a word on the topic since.

I attended a few meetings with some local community college guidance counselors, but my ongoing disinterest and opposition to being forced into further schooling prevented me from ever making any concrete decisions.

Instead, I busied myself with scanning the help wanted ads that cluttered the classified section of the daily newspaper like blackbirds on a street-side powerline.

I didn't see much of Gauge. When he wasn't inside his aunt's garage toiling away countless hours tinkering on the Indian, he was off at his new job bussing tables at a nearby restaurant. I resisted the temptation to knock on the garage door when I knew he was inside working. Many nights, I would sneak out of the house and creep alongside Aunt Mert's large aluminum garage door just to listen to the noise within. The sound of Gauge softly singing along to the radio or sporadically conversing with himself was as soothing and comforting as it was painful. I missed him, desperately so, yet I remained steadfast in my avoidance of him.

A part of me was upset that he had yet to try to see me, but I knew he was only obeying my request for distance. At least, that is what I told myself. Some nights, I would stoop beside the garage door for more than an hour, lost to the sounds of Gauge's world within, only the stinging of mosquitos or a passing car to break my drug-like trance.

The internal chatter of my mind suddenly ceased as I saw Aunt Mert cruise her giant Cadillac into her driveway. Immediately, I rose to disappear into the house before she could see me, when I heard her shout my name.

"Hey, Dustin!" she chirped in her Midwestern twang, slamming shut the massive car door.

I froze in place, contemplating an escape, yet fully aware that it was now too late to disappear without seeming rude and obvious.

Slowly, I turned to face her.

"Hey, Aunt Mert," I called back, hoping the simple hello would end the conversation.

"Won'tcha give me a hand with these groceries, hun?" she shouted in a sweet tone, her arms now full with the brown paper contents of her trunk.

Looking back at the house, ensuring that my mother wasn't spying from any windows, I tiptoed my way to Aunt Mert. The Florida sun had baked the pavement to an untouchable temperature. The skin of my upper foot and toes stung from the scorch of the ground.

"Here we go, my dear," she sang as she placed two overstuffed supermarket bags into my arms. The additional weight lowered me further onto the sizzling sidewalk, the fast-moving pain of the burn shooting through my legs and into my brain like an unexpected lightning bolt.

"Oh, my poor dear!" she laughed as she realized my barefoot dilemma. "Here," she continued, stepping back to allow me a pathway, "run into the house."

Following her direction without thought, I dashed up the driveway and to the front door. The cool relief of the shaded brick pathway that surrounded the front stoop alleviated the stinging pang of the heat and allowed me to catch my forgotten breath.

Aunt Mert appeared behind me, her giggling endearing yet slightly annoying.

"You are such a sweetheart," she laughed. "I am so sorry for making you cross all this way without your shoes on!"

She looked down at my feet as if expecting to see flames.

"You are a Florida boy! You know better than to prance around outdoors without your shoes during the summer!"

She looked up at me, waiting for the connection of our eyes.

"Didn't your mother teach you that?"

The mention of my mother streaked a flash of uncertainty and anxiety across my face like the first wave of a returning tide.

Aunt Mert saw it immediately.

"What is it, Dustin?" she asked, shifting the brown paper bags against her hips. "I could tell something was the matter the other day in the garage, and I certainly see it now."

She inched closer to me, her familiar lilac perfume accenting the air around us.

"You can talk to me, hun."

I burst into tears without warning or hesitation. The drops fell from my eyes as though someone had punctured my lower lids. I dropped to the stoop, the grocery bags hugging me like misshapen pillows.

"Oh dear," Aunt Mert whispered, placing her bags on the ground before lifting the ones from my grip. "Now, now," she spoke softly, sitting beside me, wrapping her pale arms over my shoulders like two angelic wings.

"I'm sorry," I managed through my sobbing, my mouth covered in teardrops and snot. "I'm okay, really. I'm sorry."

"Hey," Aunt Mert stated loudly, allowing her voice to override my rambling. "You listen here, dear boy. There is something clearly the matter, and I will not have you crying like a baby at my doorstep without you telling me what it is."

I looked to the ground, the site of an ant trail pulling my attention. How I wished I were that small, the troubles and stress of my human life forgotten, my existence now simple and minuscule alongside the instinctual march of millions.

"I'm fine, Aunt Mert, really."

My lie dropped from my lips as heavy and hollow as a falling, dead tree trunk. Aunt Mert wasn't buying a second of it.

"Dustin," she said sternly, placing her hand beneath my chin, pulling my face toward hers. "Talk to me."

I inhaled, the fury of words collecting on top of my tongue like bullets in a gun barrel. For the next ten minutes, I detailed the two encounters with my mother, revealing every hurtful word and angry snarl. Aunt Mert listened silently, her eyes tender and still as my hapless story washed around her like a swarm of wasps, each sentence stinging deeper than the last, each revelation more painful than the first. When I was finished, she merely stood to her feet, brushed off her blue cotton skirt, and lowered her hand toward me.

"Come," she said, her voice still and gentle. "Let's go inside."

For the next half an hour, I helped Aunt Mert unpack her lot and prepare her pre-dinner contents. She spoke of Milwaukee and her ex-husband. She chatted lightly about her beloved brother, Gauge's father, allowing her words to flow with the certainty and smoothness of tender memory. I listened on bated breath, completely absorbing her story like a fallen bread crumb on a park pond. I knew the purpose of the conversation was to distract me from my own pain, and it worked, but the content of her pointless chatter was both soothing and interesting to me. Hearing of Gauge's family history, especially of his father, was not only intriguing and exciting but also comforting, as if the mention of the fallen man was some spiritual conjuring of peace and serenity. Perhaps it was only my emotional exhaustion, but I enjoyed the feeling of both.

"Listen," she said in a more earnest and serious tone. "Your mother loves you, Dustin."

I looked at her, stunned by the clarity and beauty of her pale blue eyes.

"She is only scared for you. She doesn't know Gauge, and she is only trying to protect you. That's her job, you know. She is your mother."

I shook my head.

"No, Aunt Mert. It's more than that. It isn't about Gauge. It's about all of it. She will never accept something like this."

Aunt Mert dropped what she was doing and made her way to me.

"Dustin," she whispered, her warm breath heavy with the smell of peppermint. "She loves you. Give it time."

I closed my eyes, wishing what she said were true, though deep within me a voice confirmed that it was not.

"Please," I said, placing my hands on hers. "Please don't tell Gauge about any of this. I don't want him to be upset."

Aunt Mert smiled, her eyes filled with security and strength.

"Of course not, dear," she said, moving her hands to softly tap my cheeks. "You only tell him what you see fit."

She shuffled back to her place before the dinner ingredients.

"Though, I must say, if my Gauge were to fancy gentlemen the way you do, I would certainly be pleased if he were taken with such a sweet, fine young man such as yourself."

I blushed, lowering my head in embarrassment.

"It will all work out as it is meant to. I promise you that."

Before I could reply, the slamming of the garage door echoed from the hallway, the sound preceding the sudden appearance of Gauge.

"Hey," he said, his eyes locking with mine, a look of confusion and uncertainty gripping his expression.

"Oh...hey, love!" Aunt Mert called to him, immediately moving toward him for an embrace. I could tell her movement was to quietly subside the sudden cloud of awkwardness that now filled the kitchen like the mist of a rainforest.

"Dustin was kind enough to help me with the groceries," she continued, pulling Gauge's pack from his shoulder and placing it on the counter beside her. "We were just chatting about how things were back in Wisconsin. I told Dustin how cold it gets. I don't think his pretty little Florida self would ever stand a chance at surviving a winter up there!"

She laughed at her own joke, her voice slightly tense with an uncomfortable nervousness.

Gauge smiled at her before reconnecting his gaze with mine. Like the bursting of the universe, a plethora of unspoken words filled the space between us as enormous and powerful as a supernova.

"So, how was work, dear?" Aunt Mert questioned, forcing her words into the intensity of the energy between us. "Make any big tips today?"

"It was all right," Gauge responded, moving to the sink. He kept his eyes focused on his hands as he washed them. I allowed my eyes to trail the floor in resistance to the palpable awkwardness. So much of me wanted to jump from my chair and run to him, but just a bit more of me kept me seated in place.

Gauge moved from the sink and back to his bag. Aunt Mert and I observed in an uncertain silence as he shuffled the contents of the pack until he located a portable cassette player and headphones. He paused, keeping his face aimed toward his hands, and then slowly turned to face his eager audience.

"So, how've you been?" he asked, keeping his eyes focused on the electronic device that he fumbled in his grasp. "Haven't seen ya for a while."

I swallowed, my throat suddenly hollow and dry. My pulse began to race as I struggled to locate the use of my vocal chords.

"Good," I coughed, clearing my throat as the stuttered response fell from my lips. "Just trying to find some work and stuff. Looking into school."

A warm, comforting sense of ease fell over my skin like a familiar blanket as I felt Gauge lift his eyes to mine. My breathing became stunted and shallow as I searched for more words to ease the silence with.

"Cool," he replied, keeping his eyes firmly connected. "I've missed seeing ya around."

He turned to look at Aunt Mert, who had quietly returned to preparing her vegetables. From the position of my chair, I could see that she was smiling.

"Well," Gauge announced, "I guess I better hit the shower."

He lifted his arms to smell his armpits.

"Bussing tables has a way of making ya sweat."

I chuckled, lowering my head as he walked by.

I remained still and silent as I heard him move into the distance of the house. It was only when Aunt Mert began to continue her colorful recollections of Wisconsin did I dare to rise from the chair.

Moving to join her at the cutting board, I accepted the duty of slicing tomatoes as she fervently pounded out a collection of chicken breasts. I began to fade into my own thoughts, the sound of her non-stop speaking lulling me into a trance while the beat of the knife as it sliced the board hypnotized my thinking. It wasn't until Aunt Mert tugged at my shirt did I resume my place in reality.

"I wanted them sliced, dear, not diced," she teased, moving my attention toward the cutting board with her eyes.

"Oh, sorry. I just got a bit carried away."

"It's quite fine, my love. I am just appreciative of the help."

She moved past me, the waft of her lilac scent eliminating the smell of the fresh tomatoes that covered my fingertips.

"Now," she continued, "I need you to take this back to Gauge and tell him that dinner will be ready in fifteen minutes."

She shoved Gauge's worn navy-green knapsack into my tomato-juice-covered hands.

"But—"

"Ah, no buts," she declared, turning my shoulders with her hands. "You just go on and tell him."

I stood still, completely frozen as if attempting to conceal my existence from a prowling grizzly bear.

"Also, tell him that you will be joining us."

I thought to protest but instead found my feet moving from the kitchen and into the hallway. Before I could gather any thought or nervous fear, I was standing at Gauge's closed bedroom door, the dim light of his bedside lamp glowing through the crack between the floor and door like a beacon in the night.

My heart pounded its rhythmic drum so loudly in my ears that I could barely hear the command of my brain as it urged me to lift my arm and knock on the door.

Just as I was about to do so, an arm grabbed me from behind and spun me in a complete circle. The pack dropped to the floor as Gauge wrapped his hands around each of my wrists, lifting my arms above my head and against the closed bedroom door.

I stared in wonder as I watched his face close in, his body still wet from the shower, an off-white towel wrapped tight around his waist. I swear that my heart stopped beating as he pressed his lips to mine, the taste of his mouth warm from the heat of the shower water.

He pulled back, his face slightly illuminated by the distant light of the kitchen doorway. I could see his dark eyes as they appeared to spin in the shadows. I felt his heartbeat as he pressed himself against me, his lips touching my ear. My breath escaped as he dropped my wrists and moved his hands to cup my face. I could hear the struggle of his breathing as he again connected his soft lips with mine.

This time, the warm glide of his tongue slid over my mouth and into the space beyond my lips. The taste of Colgate toothpaste replaced the memory of Jack Daniel's that defined our first similar encounter.

I felt my body begin to drift down the door. Gauge pulled me forward, our open mouths still connected, moving us to the wall across from his bedroom. The kissing became more passionate, more intense. I wasn't sure if I was still breathing.

Somewhere in the distance, there was movement, slow but steady. We both turned our heads to see a shadowed figure staring at us. An icy layer of terror solidified over my aroused flesh as I recognized the identity of the stranger. It was my mother, her eyes wide, her mouth twisted in horror.

"Mom?" I gasped, my disbelief matching hers.

"I knew it," she growled, reaching her arm for the wall. "I knew this was going on. That's why I just let myself in. I wanted to see the truth."

She clutched her chest and fell against the wall, closing her eyes and resting in place. I moved toward her as she struggled to breathe.

"Mom!" I cried, gripping her sunken shoulders with both hands.

"No!" she screamed, every ounce of her strength bellowing from her throat as she launched from the wall.

I saw a flash of red as her closed fist slammed against my head. I opened my eyes just in time to see the other fist hurling toward my eye. I fell to the floor as she struck me, lifting her body like a wildcat onto my upper frame. I saw Gauge scrambling to reach us as I fell, my head landing on the wooden floorboards with a bouncing thud. The scratching of her fingernails singed and burned my flesh like heated steel branding a cattle's backside. The sensation of her saliva as it showered over my face stung like acid rain, her clenched fists opening to grip my neck. She began to tighten her hands, when she was lifted into the air.

From the darkened haze of my clouded vision, I saw Gauge holding my mother above me, her arms flailing like some wild creature materialized from the conjuring of the devil. I began to taste the blood that trickled from the open wounds clawed across my face. The lingering sensation of Gauge's tongue was replaced by the coating thickness of my own blood. In an instant, a moment of unexpected ecstasy had darkened and morphed into a nightmarish reality. I struggled to lift myself from the floor when I heard my mother break free from Gauge's grasp, scrambling her way across the floor like a crab escaping a fisherman's net.

She pounced on me just as I was inching myself up the wall, dragging me back to the floorboards with the pounding of her balled fists. I could hear both Gauge and Aunt Mert crying out as they struggled to pull the raging woman from on top of me. Though I knew I could try to resist her, I didn't move. I simply lay still as my mother unleashed her fearful terror onto my body.

Tears began to intermingle with blood as both liquids seeped across my skin. It wasn't until I heard Aunt Mert's voice as she gripped my shoulders that I realized that my mother had again been removed. The blasting assault of her limbs had become so fevered and constant that my nerves began to dull and paralyze to the pain of her blows.

I opened my eyes to see Aunt Mert carefully pulling my body toward her. I felt my face stick to her blouse as the coated mixture of blood, tears, and saliva pressed into the neatly ironed garment. In the distance, I could hear Gauge attempting to calm my mother.

"Get off of me, you sick piece of shit!" she snarled. "Look what you've done to my son! Look what you've done to my boy!"

Her words curled over my wounds like streaks of vinegar. The sound of her voice stung and irritated my battle-wounded flesh like salt over a slug's back.

Aunt Mert slid me into the bathroom, closing the door behind her. The echoing drone of my mother shouting insults at Gauge filled the space around us like thunder over a mountain range. Aunt Mert began to crack corny jokes in an attempt to distract me as she slowly dabbed a warm washcloth over my face. I didn't speak as she cleaned me, wiping the blood from my skin as if it were no more unusual than the tomato juice I had splattered over her kitchen cutting board just moments ago.

It was then that the bathroom door flew open, my mother hunched in the doorframe, her hair matted, her face blackened with dirt, debris, and blood. Gauge trailed behind her, gripping her shoulders before she could enter the small space between us.

"I have just one thing to say to you," she stated in between labored breaths. "If this is the life you want, if these are the people you want to live it with...then you just go ahead and live it."

She forced herself out from under Gauge's grasp.

"But know this, my boy," she continued, her voice darkening with the shadows in her eyes. "You no longer have a mother if this is who you choose to be."

She glared at me, two tears streaming in unison down her cheeks like falling stars hurled from the universe. No one moved. Everyone could only stare, the shock and disbelief of the entire encounter too cumbersome for our brains to compute and process.

Wiping her face, my mother turned and moved out from under Gauge's arm and into the darkness of the hallway. I watched Gauge's face as he carefully observed her movement beyond what Aunt Mert and I could see within the confines of the bathroom. He moved to follow her, leaving only the gaping black hole of the doorway as evidence to the nightmare. We heard muffled voices before the slamming of the front door.

"Now, you listen here," Aunt Mert spoke directly into my face. "You just rest and stop thinking about all this while I get you cleaned up."

She moved to the sink to refresh the washcloth. I could see the clouded water as she wrung out the fabric, the collection of my tear-soaked blood pouring from the rag like streams of diluted oil. It took several more cleansings before Aunt Mert felt satisfied with her effort. Slowly, she assisted me to my feet, inching me toward the doorway. I glanced in the mirror as we moved, the reflection of my bruised and battered face staring back at me as broken and pathetic as my current self-worth. My swollen eyes peered at me as if from the face of some outer space creature. My lips looked like two undercooked sausages, massive and sliced with a series of abrasions that streaked across the tender flesh like the markings of a serpent. I was tempted to collapse in tears, but the firm grip of Aunt Mert's lead was stronger than my weakened impulses.

She shuffled me across the hall and into Gauge's room. As she lowered me onto the bed, I stretched my sore and bruised body over the bedsheets as though the coolness of the linen could somehow heal my wounds. I closed my eyes as Aunt Mert worked to tuck me in, lifting my head so that she could insert a pillow. The smell of Gauge's skin and hair streamed into my nostrils like a warm breeze caressing the frozen Arctic tundra. I pressed my face deeper into the pillow, the familiar scent heightening my ability to smell above the stressed churning of my four other senses. For just a moment, the throbbing pain of my cuts and bruises subsided, with only the familiar presence of Gauge occupying my sluggish consciousness.

"Try and get some rest, dear," she said softly, brushing hair back from my forehead. "We will figure all of this out in the morning."

A tear escaped my left eye as she gently kissed my scalp, her maternal kindness as keen as if I were her kin. I closed my eyes as she exited the room, no thought or memory of what had just occurred polluting my mind.

Just as I was fading into the haze of slumber, a presence beside me alerted my awareness. I jumped into a sitting position, the wailing of my abrasions jolting through my being like electricity. I sat up to see Gauge.

"Hey," he whispered, his eyes glossy, his face captive to an expression I had yet to see on him. "Are you okay?"

I nodded, too exhausted to speak.

"I'm so sorry, Dustin," he continued, dropping to his knees so that we were eye level. "For everything. I shouldn't have done that. I shouldn't have let—"

"Stop, Gauge," I mumbled, my throat still tight from where my mother had been choking me. "This isn't your fault. None of it is. You didn't do anything wrong."

"It's just..." he stopped.

I looked up to see him wiping away tears.

"You do something to me. Something about you makes me feel something that I can't explain...or even understand."

I didn't react as I watched him struggle for more words.

"I can't control it. It isn't right. I shouldn't just act out this way."

"I love you," I stated, as certain and strong as though I were reciting my name.

He looked up at me, tears wavering over his confused gaze. "What?"

"I love you, Gauge. I have for weeks. Since we met. Since that first time you took me to the lake."

I reached down, placing my hand onto his.

"So nothing you have done is wrong. I feel the same way."

The swell of tears slipped from his eyes and down his cheeks. His bottom lip began to quiver, his breathing accelerated and slightly labored.

"No, Dustin," he struggled through his tears. "This isn't right."

"How is it not right?" I retorted, my frustration as apparent as the sliced nail marks across my face. "If it's what you feel, then it is real. How can it be wrong? You didn't choose it. I didn't choose it. It just is."

He kept his head down, droplets of water falling from his face like a leaking water spot on a rain-weary ceiling.

"To say it's wrong," I continued, moving my arms to my chest, "it makes you sound just like my mother."

"No," he replied, placing both hands over mine. "That's not how I mean it. I just mean—"

"What, Gauge? What do you mean?"

He stared, my angered interruption both unexpected and startling.

"Because I am getting so tired of people telling me what's right and wrong for me. No one knows what I feel. No one knows what it's like to just feel something so strong, so powerful, that it consumes you. Even when you sleep. It's the easiest and most natural thing I have ever felt, yet I am constantly being told it is wrong. I can't listen to that anymore."

"I—" he cut himself off, his eyes darting between mine as if begging for an answer.

"Say it, Gauge," I shouted. "Say it because I can't keep dealing with you saying things one way but acting in another."

He didn't blink as his gaze continued to labor with tears. I could feel his fingers as he nervously prodded at my skin.

"I don't know. I don't know what it is," he stammered, continuing to search my face with his eyes as if desperate to find his answer there. "I understand what you mean, though. When you say you feel it even when you sleep. I understand that. That's what it's like for me."

"That's love, Gauge," I whispered, my voice giving way to my own tears.

He smiled before dropping his head, the chatter of his brain nearly audible within the inches between us.

"We need to get you out of here," he said, lifting his face. "You can't stay here anymore."

"What?" I asked softly, my head aching with a relentless throbbing.

"Your mother...she's out of her mind. You can't stay here with her."

"Don't worry," I replied, leaning my pulsating skull against the headboard. "This will blow over. She'll calm down."

"Do you hear yourself? Dustin, look at me."

I opened my eyes and turned my head to face him.

"This is abuse. I know you are grown, but this is crazy, man. She was beating you."

I sighed, reclosing my eyes as I positioned my head on the pillow.

"It will be fine," I attempted to assure him, my words no more stable than a palm frond in a hurricane.

"No, Dustin. It isn't fine. None of this is."

Gauge gripped my shoulders, gently turning me toward him.

"I want to take you out of here," he said, his face only inches from mine. "Let's go to LA. Let's just go."

"Gauge," I laughed, the constant beat of my heart the barometer for my pain. "How are we going to do that? With what money?"

"I've got savings," he responded immediately, his expression brightening. "It's money my dad left. It's a few grand. It could get us to California."

I shook my head, closing my eyes.

"I mean it, Dustin. Let's just go."

"And what will we do when we get there, Gauge?" I asked, lifting my head from the pillow. "What do you think, we will just waltz into Hollywood and I will land some great acting gig and everything will be fine?"

He stared at me, his eyes sinking with the weight of my words.

"I've only done a few high school plays. I'm no actor, Gauge. This is all your fantasy. It's just something I say, it's not something I really mean."

He looked hurt, as though I had just revealed to his six-year-old self that there wasn't a Santa Claus.

"But you wanted to swim in the Pacific," he replied, his voice seasoned with confusion. "I want to be able to do that for you...to get you there. I want to see you have your dream."

"Gauge," I sighed, replacing my head on the pillow. "It's not a big deal. The ocean is the ocean. I will survive if I never swim in the Pacific."

I kept my eyes closed as he inched away, returning to his feet and moving to the door.

"This really sucks to hear you talk this way," he said from the doorway. "To see you just give up on everything."

I didn't speak. Instead, I focused on my breathing as I struggled not to lash out at him. Though I appreciated his endearing sincerity, now was not the time for me to talk about far-fetched dreams regarding crossing the country to chase acting aspirations or Pacific Ocean waves. Instead, I just wanted to sleep.

"You may be right," he continued, his voice now steady and certain, "about how I feel and everything."

I opened my eyes to see his face.

"I don't really know how to put all this stuff into words, but I think you're right."

His soft face glowed in the faint light of the bedside lamp, his eyes the familiar jewels of my dreams.

"I just know that I wanna be with you. Always."

He left the room, closing the door quietly behind him.

The enormity of it all pressed upon my chest like fallen boulders in a forgotten canyon. So much of me wanted to weep, for the physical pain, the psychological tyranny, and now, the emotional exuberance. I fell asleep knowing that Gauge loved me in the same way that I loved him. This alone was enough to ease my heart and coo my brain into a silent, restful sleep.

II.

1984

S IX MONTHS HAD PASSED SINCE GAUGE AND I LEFT FLORIDA. The night after the altercation with my mother, Gauge secured his savings, which was far less than the few grand he was expecting, and we boarded the Indian and headed north. With only the clothing on our backs, we slipped into the night without witness. Gauge left Aunt Mert a note with the promise to contact her once we reached a more secure destination. He was hell-bent on making it to California as soon as possible, but the Indian had other plans.

We traveled as far as Atlanta, Georgia, when the alternator gave out. Luckily, my cousin Ruby lived just over the state line in Tennessee and was willing to retrieve us. We stayed with her and her boyfriend for about three weeks, until we attained a place of our own, a tiny room at the back of a run-down yet still fully functional highway-side motel. I worked housekeeping for the motel while Gauge found a part-time position as a mechanic's apprentice at a nearby repair garage.

Between the two of us, we earned a meager living, a non-operational motorcycle and a few hundred dollars in a mason jar our only fortune.

I never contacted my parents after we left, nor did I inform them of my leaving. After listening to Gauge insist that we escape our hopeless entrapment in South Florida, I agreed to disappear with him into the night, uncaring as to where we were going or how we would get there. As long as I was with him, I was content.

Our place at the motel was smaller than my bedroom back home. We managed, though, not only in the practical sense, but our connection flourished as well. Eight hours a day of scrubbing corroded toilets was worth the sacrifice just to be able to lie beside Gauge each night.

The first time we made love, I wept in silence, my tears intermeshed with the sweat of our tangled bodies. There was no talk or hesitation, it simply happened as if it had occurred a thousand times before. As the months progressed, our sexual chemistry evolved, becoming more rhythmic and fluid. In time, we were as familiar with each other's bodies as we were our own, easily able to connect and satisfy the other without effort or thought.

It turned out that the Indian required more work than we had originally anticipated. Gauge spent a large portion of his remaining savings moving us into the motel, a rent that was now a fraction of the original amount due to my on-site employment. Nearly the rest of what was left was spent on the Indian, which was now no more functional than it had been when it stranded us in Georgia.

Still, we were happy. We planned to get the bike going again and continue our westbound dream, but I had accepted the present fate of our circumstance a few weeks after we settled into the motel and I saw that Gauge was getting nowhere with the repairs. When he wasn't busy at the garage, he was home tinkering on the Indian, its mechanical parts and pieces carefully spread over one of the motel bedsheets in the alleyway across from the dumpsters.

The motel manager, a grossly overweight man named Mr. Higgins, wasn't so keen on Gauge, his tattoos, or his endless laboring on the Indian, but he accepted it, as I was one of the few of his employees who actually showed up on a daily basis and never ended my shift early due to an unintentional drug-induced collapse on one of the bathroom floors. I minded my manners and kept to myself, dutifully repeating my daily tasks like a worker bee on a singular mission.

Most of my days were spent changing the cum-stained bedsheets where truckers had sexually ravaged one of the local hookers or repeatedly pleasured themselves with the guidance and aide of the sole VHS smut film Mr. Higgins played on a loop from the motel's office. We were the only motel within a seventy-mile radius with a VCR, and its ability to display the same hour-long adult film into every room was more than likely the only reason the motel was still in business.

Thankfully, Gauge was a naturally gifted cook. He could take the simplest of ingredients and construct the most basic yet delicious meals. They weren't always attractive or all that appetizing when you broke down the ingredients, but they satiated hunger, and their distinct and captivating flavors would be the envy of any honest culinary artist.

Soups made of condiments and enhanced with spices, or dried noodle delicacies mixed with meager portions of convenience store meat, we never went hungry and were somehow always able to enjoy our limited intake by the grace of Gauge's creative genius.

Tonight was special, so I was planning an evening out. For weeks I had been setting aside a bit of extra funds so that I could surprise Gauge with a birthday dinner out on the town. There wasn't much to choose from in our backwoods, rural location, but there was one Italian restaurant in the heart of the county that people raved about for miles. It was rumored that Frank Sinatra himself once graced the joint during his glorious heyday with the Rat Pack. Of course, there was no photographic evidence of this rare and grand occurrence, but the legend persisted as strongly as the blue smoke of the nearby Appalachian Mountains.

Over the months, we managed to collect a resourceful yet slightly fashionable wardrobe. Having arrived with nothing but the clothing we had on, Mr. Higgins connected us with one of the dozens of nearby churches where we were able to obtain some charitable gear. I was both surprised and amused at how current and relevant some of the donated clothing was. My only guess was that some of the strict, religious parents had confiscated some of their children's modern, rock and roll "sin wear" and purged their homes of it via a charitable, church-funded donation.

I carefully ironed the best of our garments, a pair of black slacks and a white button-down dress shirt for me, and a denim jean and jacket combo for Gauge. Touring the room with my eyes, a sudden wave of gratitude washed over me as warm as the Caribbean Sea. Given the unexpected and stark contrast of our present reality, especially compared to where we had come from, Gauge and I were far more equipped to not only survive and continue on, but also to enjoy the bit of life we had accumulated and created. Things could be so much worse, and I was sincerely grateful to the gods above that they weren't.

The rattling of keys broke my stream of daydream thoughts. Gauge appeared in the room, black and filthy with the grease, gunk, and grime of the repair shop.

"Hey," he said as he closed the door behind him, his familiar, crooked smile revealing a pearly white set of teeth beneath the darkened mask of his face. "What'cha doin?"

"I have a surprise for you, birthday boy," I replied, moving in to kiss him. "Get cleaned up. I am taking you to Mazzola's."

He stared at me a moment, the confusion and uncertainty of his brain spinning in his eyes like a tumbling dryer load.

"Wait," he continued, his expression more concerned than excited. "Mazzola's? That fancy Italian place in town where Frank Sinatra ate?"

I nodded, my grin as big as the full moon.

"Babe, no," he said, shaking his head. "We can't afford something like that. I'm fine just hanging out here tonight. What's another birthday? I'm a grown man now. It ain't no big thing."

"Nonsense, Gauge," I stated, a smile still glued to my face as I helped lift his sweat and grease-covered work shirt over his head. "I've been saving for this for weeks. It's something I want to do."

I placed my hands on his cheeks, ensuring that his eyes were fixed on mine.

"It's something we need to do."

He nodded silently, unbuckling his belt and removing his pants. The sight of Gauge without clothing was still the most erotic and exciting image to me. The naturally toned curvature of his body, every inch of his skin, the hair, the ink markings, it was all an endless stream of sensory fantasy that I was able to hold in my arms each and every night.

I watched as he trotted off toward the bathroom, his taut and compact butt appearing to wave at me as he walked by.

Mr. Higgins had given me permission to take one of his service trucks into town. He kept two rundown old Chevy pickups on-site to manage the retrieval of motel goods. He bulk-purchased via some sketchy wholesale warehouse nearby and would often send me to fetch the orders in an attempt to save on delivery fees.

Once we were both showered and dressed in our best, we loaded into the nude-colored Chevy and started toward Mazzola's.

The truck radio murmured one of the many old-timey country music stations of the area, the mournful sound of Patsy Cline's powerful voice filling the cabin like a welcome springtime cloud.

After around forty minutes of driving, we pulled into a crowded parking lot that hugged a quaint old wooden-framed building.

A bright and massive flashing sign dominated the front of the structure like a lighthouse on the edge of a tiny beachside pier. The words "Mazzola's Homestyle Italian Cuisine" blared across the surrounding asphalt like the sun illuminating the moon.

I pulled the rattling truck into one of the available spaces. Hopping out, we journeyed through the jungle of dust-covered, big-wheeled pickups and family station wagons toward the front of the restaurant.

The intense and unmistakable aroma of classic Italian food wrapped itself around us as we moved into the tiny entryway.

A sea of trucker caps, cowboy hats, and church lady bouffant hairdos sprouted above the brown panel half-wall that stood between us and the rest of the patrons.

"Well, good evening, boys," a cheerful Southern accent chirped. "Y'all here together, or are there gonna be more of ya comin?"

A small, white-haired man shuffled toward us with a stack of menus in his hands. He wore a black tailcoat over what appeared to be a worn and stained undershirt. His black pants were baggy and loose-fitted, appearing as though they had been a tailored fit back in his more primitive years.

"No, just us," I answered, hugging up to Gauge's side.

The old man peered at us suspiciously a moment before replacing his stare with a warm and inviting smile.

"Well, then, right this way, gentlemen."

He led us through the chattering hoard of hungry diners toward a small, white-cloth-covered table in the very back of the restaurant.

A small candle in a chipped glass next to a red plastic flower in a white, bumpy vase split the table in two.

Once seated, the man listed an array of house specials before disappearing behind a nearby red-checkered curtain.

We were busy perusing our prolific menus when our waitress greeted us.

"Well, howdy, fellas," she stated joyously, her bleached blonde hair teased and stretched over her head like an off-white cotton headdress, her pale blue eyeshadow caked thick behind spiderlike lashes. A streak of red lipstick stained her brilliantly white teeth, their perfect, symmetrical shape making it obvious that they were dentures.

"What can I get ya handsome young men to drink?" she continued, whipping out a worn notepad and pen.

"I'll have a Coke," I replied, Gauge following suit.

"Two Cokes it is," she smiled, replacing the notepad into her apron pocket.

"Y'all visiting, or are ya from around here?" she questioned, bouncing her mascara-clouded eyes between us.

"We moved nearby about six months ago," I answered, smiling up at her.

"Oh, nice. Where y'all from originally?"

"South Florida," I continued, "but it was getting too hot and muggy, so we wanted to venture north."

She laughed.

"Too hot and muggy? Well, honey, you need to keep heading north if you intend to escape the hot and muggy. Tennessee gets as hot and stale as a mule's behind for about eight months of the year."

The three of us laughed in unison.

"Y'all brothers or something?"

"No," I replied, looking at Gauge.

"High school buddies?" she queried, the singsong tone of her voice now becoming more curious and inquisitive.

"Boyfriends," I stated, returning my gaze to her.

"Oh," she said, her powdered face flushed with a hint of crimson. "I see."

She continued to stare a moment before seeming to collect her distracted thoughts.

"Well, I'll be right back."

She turned slowly, her white leather short-heeled shoes scraping the carpet as she moved. I watched as she glanced back at us before disappearing behind the checkered curtain.

"Now why did you have to go and tell her that?" Gauge questioned, his voice whispered yet concerned.

"What do you mean?" I asked. "It's the truth, isn't it?"

"Well, yeah, I guess so, but that doesn't mean we need to tell the hillbilly waitress."

He turned his head to scan the rest of the crowded dining room.

"Saying shit like that can get you killed in a ho-dunk place like this."

I lowered my head in a mixture of shame and frustration. A part of me was embarrassed for upsetting Gauge, but the rest of me was annoyed that he seemed to care so much about what a complete stranger thought of us.

Before I could reply, a heavyset man in a pale pink shirt with an offensively clashing red tie approached the table.

"I'm gonna have to ask you boys to leave," he stated coldly in a thick Southern drawl.

"What?" I croaked, my voice heavy with confusion and shock.

"Please don't make me ask you twice."

He crossed his arms over his belly, resting them atop the protruding gut like an armrest.

I turned to look at Gauge, who was already staring at me.

"And can I ask why?" Gauge questioned, returning his eyes to the man.

"Peg, your waitress, tells me that y'all are boyfriends," he responded in the same flat tone.

"Yeah, so?" Gauge replied, his face twisting in confusion and a bit of anger.

"Well, we won't have that kind of thing in this family establishment."

The man leaned toward us, lowering his voice to say, "The Bible condemns you, and so do we."

He pulled himself back to his complete height, his arms still resting lifelessly on his giant belly.

I felt the room begin to sway as Gauge's anger boiled over. I attempted to stop him as he pushed back his chair and jumped to his feet.

"And what right do you have to condemn us, sir?" he boomed, his deep voice thundering through the restaurant like the roar of a tornado.

"As a Christian, I have the right of God on my side. This is my family's restaurant, and we can refuse service to whoever lives a life of rebellion to God."

He shot his eyes between us before sneering, "And personally, you two faggots make me sick."

I closed my eyes as I heard the thud of Gauge's fist meet the flesh of the man's face. An immediate silence fell over the entire dining room, preceded by an audible collection of gasps.

I opened my eyes to see the man pulling the clipped-on tie from his neck and throwing it to the ground. In one fell swoop, he grabbed the corners of Gauge's denim collar and pushed him toward the red-checkered curtain.

The sound of dishes and utensils falling to the floor could be heard crashing in the distance beyond what could be seen.

I jumped to my feet and began to pursue them, when Gauge reappeared from behind the curtain, his lip bleeding, his face red and swollen.

"Let's go," he commanded, grabbing my arm and pulling me toward the gathering collection of disturbed and curious onlookers.

"Wait!" a voice yelled. We turned to see the man, his face beet red from the unseen altercation. "I'm meeting you in the parking lot."

Gauge shook his head before continuing to lead us toward the door. The frightened stares of the other diners as we hurried past them was both terrifying and amusing to me. I knew they could only wonder what in the hell was happening.

Gauge threw open the restaurant door, squeezing my arm tighter as we raced for the truck.

The sound of a chain and something wooden clubbing the ground halted our movement. We turned to see the fat man, along with two equally sized counterparts, closing in on us from the side of the building.

"Go!" Gauge shouted, pushing me toward the truck. "Get in and lock the doors!"

"But—" I started, choking on my words.

"Just do it, Dustin!" he commanded, his voice shaking with emotion.

Obeying the order, I unlatched the heavy, creaking truck door and hopped inside. Locking both doors with the pound of my fist, I turned just in time to see one of the men swing a bat at Gauge's head.

I cried out as Gauge ducked, moving forward toward his original opponent, who patiently smirked at him while tightly gripping a chain.

Gauge crashed into the man's torso, knocking the solid and stout body back several inches. The two cronies closed in, and I could no longer see Gauge.

I watched in absolute horror, my heart pounding in my ears, my lungs shaking like dried leaves inside my core as the three men circled a still-crouching Gauge.

The clanking of the chains and the solid whack of the baseball bat echoed into the truck like dynamite blasting the inner belly of a rocky hollow.

Time slowed to an excruciatingly stunted crawl. What happened in seconds appeared to goop and glaze across time like a fresh and heavy sap suffocating a tree.

I felt myself begin to heave and sob as I witnessed the men drift apart, spitting and kicking at their fallen victim. In what felt like centuries, I watched them trail into the distance, returning to the building, their cheerful hooting and hollering signifying their victory.

As soon as the men were completely out of sight, I shoved open the weighted truck door and slid from the cabin.

With my vision compromised by the watery haze of my tears, I fell to the ground and crawled forward until I made out the crumpled formation of Gauge.

Wiping my eyes, I lost my breath as I took in the sight before me.

There, balled in a fetal position, was Gauge, his face completely plastered in blood, his skin already swollen, leaving only two nearly indistinguishable slits to signify where his eyes used to be.

My horrified tears returned as I threw myself on top of his freshly beaten body.

"Gauge!" I shouted, pressing my face against his, the warm coating of his blood stamping onto my flesh as though I had leaned against a giant red inkpad.

I heard him mumble, his voice distant and muffled.

"Gauge, I'm here," I cried, "I'm right here!"

I looked up to see the restaurant patrons filing out into the parking lot, their faces either frozen in shock and horror or emblazoned with peering and satisfied smirks.

I lowered my shoulder below his arm, supporting his heavy head as I pulled to lift him from the ground.

In a swift and mighty movement, I was able to lift both Gauge, who is taller and heavier than me, and myself into a standing position. I gave one last tearstained glare at our audience before turning us toward the truck.

Gauge moaned as I pushed him into the cabin, blood streaming over the cracked leather seats like rain water greeting the dry desert floor. Curling his legs beneath him, I slammed the door shut and ran to the driver's side.

"You're going to hell, faggot!" I heard a woman scream, looking up just in time to see our waitress, Peg, shouting the angry words.

Jumping into the cab, I fired up the engine and tossed the truck into reverse.

I smashed the gas, the squeaking vehicle obeying the shriek of the rubber tires as they slipped and struggled to grip the gravel of the pavement.

I turned my head as we reversed, watching the mixture of confused and hateful faces as the tailgate of the pickup neared where they stood.

I never hit the brake as I kicked the gearshift into drive, watching the screaming crowd break and disperse like a swarm of cockroaches at the flick of a light switch.

A dust-filled cloud of debris rumbled over them as I smashed the pedal, lurching the time-worn truck across the parking lot like a running bull. I guided the pickup onto the two-way county road and barreled toward home. I heard Gauge take one final staggered breath before fading into unconsciousness. Never in my life had I been so terrified. Never in my existence did I feel so dehumanized.

***

"I'LL CALL THE DOCTOR," Mr. Higgins stated after just one short glance at Gauge. "He can be hard to reach at times, but he's good. He's dependable."

"But I don't have that much money," I replied, my voice broken and hollow from constant crying. "I can pay with what's left in our savings. It's all we have, if he will take it."

Mr. Higgins stared at me a moment before shaking his head.

"Don't worry about that now," he said. "We will figure out all that later."

I returned to the bed after Mr. Higgins left the room, a still breathing but heavily unconscious Gauge bloodied, bruised, and beaten in the center of the multicolored bedspread.

I looked down at the pile of blood-soaked washcloths and towels I had used to clean him. Luckily, none of the thrash marks left by the chains seemed deep enough to produce a steady bleeding. Most of the damage appeared to be deep and internal, with the majority of the trauma suffered to the head.

I began to carefully remove the bloodstained denim jacket, when I heard Mr. Higgins return to the room.

"Lucky break, I caught him just as he was about to leave town for the night. He's going to stop by on his way."

I stared at Mr. Higgins, grateful for his kindness but uncertain as to his motives. He had made it clear to me on more than one occasion that he was not a fan of Gauge's, yet here he was, concerned and proactive as Gauge lay bleeding and unconscious all over his truck, towels, and bedspread.

"Thank you, Mr. Higgins," I sobbed, my endless stream of tears flowing as constant as Niagara Falls. "I didn't know what else to do or where to take him. I didn't even know where the nearest hospital was."

"You're better off here," he replied. "I trust this doc way more than I do any of those quacks down at the county hospital."

I nodded, relieved.

"So what exactly happened?" Mr. Higgins asked, pulling up a chair so that he could sit. I suddenly realized that I had never seen this man move as quickly or as much in the entire span of months I knew him than I had in the last fifteen minutes. The demanding physical activity had obviously taken its toll, as I heard his breathing become labored and heavy. I watched in a tearful stare as he slowly and carefully lowered himself into the small wooden chair. Once on it, he looked like a circus bear trained to sit, the folds of fat and skin hanging over the quaint furniture, both impressive and comical.

I detailed the events of the night quickly and solemnly. My voice remained calm and strong as I relived the attack, though my tears never ceased to flow.

Mr. Higgins just looked at me, the echo of my words surrounding him like a swarm of angry hornets. I continued to remove Gauge's jacket, when Mr. Higgins broke the silence.

"You guys can't stay here," he declared, his voice tense and wavered.

I turned to face him.

"What do you mean?" I asked, my pulse now as speeded as my words.

"I mean it isn't safe for you boys here," he said, a look of concern and worry now accenting his expression. "People like that...you just can't stay around here now that people know of you."

I shook my head, my heart racing, my breathing rapid and shallow.

"We have nowhere to go, Mr. Higgins," I stated through a heavier flow of tears. "We have no one or no way to leave here."

"Take the truck," he said without hesitation. "Load up the motorcycle and just get out of here."

My heart froze, and my lungs hollowed. Mr. Higgins's words fell over me, weighted and meaningless. For what felt like hours, I could only stare.

"I'll give you some money. I'll also pay the doctor. Just don't worry about all that. Just take the truck and go...as soon as you can."

I watched as his eyes drifted toward Gauge, his worried expression fading into fear and disbelief.

"Why are you doing this for us?" I choked through my tense throat.

"I'm a Christian," he announced, the declaration flashing me back to earlier in the night when the restaurant owner echoed the very same description of himself.

"And one of the things I've learned in following Christ is that you help those less fortunate," he continued, keeping his sad and wary gaze fixed on Gauge. "So, that is what I know is right."

He looked at me, his stare brimming with tears.

"The right thing to do is to help you. Regardless of anything, we are all children of God, and none of us are perfect enough to judge."

I watched in my tearful silence as he wiped his eyes.

"I ain't here to judge ya, son," he continued, replacing his glasses onto his face. "God just tells me to love my fellow man. Judge not lest ye be judged."

I stared at the man, his words and reaction a far cry from the others I had known who claimed belief and obedience to the same faith.

"Thank you," I whispered, closing my eyes as my crying became more physical and overbearing.

I sat on the bed just as a blaring car horn trumpeted in the distance.

"That'll be the doc," Mr. Higgins stated, struggling to lift himself from the chair. I moved to assist him, allowing him to press a portion of his enormous weight onto my skeleton as he slowly found his stance.

I stood behind him as he shuffled out the door and into the alleyway. He returned several minutes later with a tall, bald, thin man trailing his movement.

"Dustin, this is Dr. Marks," Mr. Higgins announced as the two men entered the room.

Dr. Marks smiled at me but did not wait for a response as he moved toward the bed.

Quickly and fluidly, he examined Gauge's head and body before reaching for the large black leather briefcase he had carried in with him.

Mr. Higgins and I stood beside each other as the doctor pulled a barrage of medical materials from the case. In what seemed like mere seconds, the man stitched, bandaged, and gauzed Gauge like a character from an old Frankenstein film.

He then stared long and hard into Gauge's dramatically swollen eyes with a small flashlight, mumbling to himself as he observed.

The doctor peered at his waiting audience as he returned to his bag, retrieving a small brown bottle before returning to the bedside.

My stomach jumped as Gauge jolted awake after Dr. Marks shoved the open bottle top into one of his nostrils.

"Good, good," the doctor murmured as Gauge continued to stir on the bed.

"Just stay put," Dr. Marks commanded without looking at us. "The boy needs space to breathe."

A whirlwind of emotion stirred inside me as I watched Gauge turn and wiggle on the bed. I resisted the urge to move toward him, out of fear of somehow interfering with his recovery. I stayed put next to Mr. Higgins as Dr. Marks continued to examine Gauge, shining the flashlight repeatedly over each eye like a police helicopter pursuing an escaped convict.

Gauge continued to animate to life over the next several minutes. Dr. Marks eventually briefed me on his condition, detailing a list of home care instructions and a hopeful prognosis.

"Keep him awake for the next hour," Dr. Marks instructed. "He has a concussion but will be fine."

He turned to face Gauge before returning his attention to me.

"It is a miracle he didn't sustain severe head trauma," he continued, his voice stern yet soothing. "Most of the damage seems to have been done to his hands. He must have shielded his head with them during the attack. We need to get some X-rays. I have a feeling we have more than a few broken bones on our hands."

He lifted his eyes and chuckled.

"That wasn't an intentional pun," he quirked, pausing for a response.

When I failed to deliver one, he turned to Mr. Higgins and nodded.

"Frank," he said, "see these boys to Sandhill General. I'll call in the X-rays. Let's do what's needed, and I'll contact you later about the bill."

Dr. Marks kneeled to retrieve his case, took one final look at Gauge, and then turned to leave.

"Gentlemen," he said, smiling from the door. "The hospital will take care of the rest."

"Thank you, Dr. Marks," I piped in meekly. "Thank you so much for coming here."

The doctor stared at me, clearly assessing my presence as he carefully scanned over my face with his birdlike eyes.

"My pleasure, young man," he smiled, turning the knob and disappearing into the night.

Mr. Higgins and I carefully loaded Gauge into Mr. Higgins's powder-blue Pontiac sedan. Gauge mumbled some words at me as we gently laid him in the massive backseat of the car. I kissed his hands before closing the door, the temporary break in my tears ending as I took in the sight of his bruised, swollen, and slightly mangled knuckles and fingers. It was obvious, even to the untrained eye, that both hands were badly injured and broken.

I lowered myself carefully into the other side of the car, lifting Gauge's head onto my lap as if it were made of tissue-thin crystal.

His familiar dark eyes gleamed up at me, swallowed tight within the swollen mass of his skin.

"Hey," I whispered into his face. "You stay awake for me, okay?"

He nodded, his battered lips slowly forming his signature crooked smile.

He blinked as several of my teardrops splashed over his beaten face like a midnight rain.

I wiped them away and kissed his brow as Mr. Higgins peeled into the night.

***

TWO WEEKS LATER, WE were in New Mexico, just outside the small town of Cuervo. The hospital had only kept Gauge long enough to perform the X-rays, set and cast his broken bones, and complete the endless task of cleaning and bandaging the areas Dr. Marks had missed. Once complete, we were asked to leave, our lack of insurance or upfront payment a leading concern for the hospital.

Between the generosity of Mr. Higgins and Dr. Marks, the entire visit was paid for, though only the bare minimum was approved, as we were back out on the street in less than three hours.

Mr. Higgins brought us home, where I packed and situated our entire lives into the old Chevy pickup. Mr. Higgins handed me a small white envelope with four hundred dollars cash, along with a handwritten note stating that he authorized me to take the vehicle. I wasn't sure if it was legal or not, but I was grateful for the gesture.

Gauge slept for most of the first day of driving. The hospital allowed him a few days' worth of painkillers, so I dispersed them to him sparingly. Both hands obtained severe fractures, perhaps nerve damage, along with a broken elbow and two bruised ribs. He looked so meek and helpless beneath the mass of plaster casts and gauze. It was obvious that he was not going to be able to work once we reached California, but I promised myself that I wouldn't dwell on the dire circumstances until we arrived there. For now, I simply enjoyed the scenic trek across the country, taking in highways over landscapes I had only seen on television or in pictures. The desert was breathtaking and so alien to me. Having only known South Florida all my life, anything other than palm trees, golf courses, and mosquito-infested swamps was exotic.

Along the way, we slept in the truck, the two of us crammed inside the tiny cabin like opossums in a den. I always made sure that the thickest and best blanket was wrapped tightly around Gauge, leaving myself with a collection of T-shirts and motel towels for covering.

The desert was cold at night, something I was unaware of. Several times, I found myself waking to the rattling vibration of my teeth as they clattered inside my skull. I would press my body into Gauge's, who seemed to always sleep soundly, ensuring that he was warm until the dawn.

After two and a half days on the road, we reached New Mexico, our journey's end. The Chevy provided its share of fits and trouble along the way, but we were always able to keep moving. Less than one hundred miles beyond the state line, the beat-up truck sputtered its dissatisfaction with its labor for the very last time. Miraculously, the final acceleration rolled us off the highway and into a gas station parking lot. Next to it, a cheap roadside motel.

The Desert Star was no fancier than the dump we had just left behind, but it certainly provided a much warmer and secure night than the truck cabin.

After paying for a two-nights' stay, I unloaded Gauge and our belongings into the room, even wheeling in the Indian out of fear it would be stolen in the night.

At this point, Gauge was more lucid, therefore, in far more pain. I divvied out his last remaining pain pills and watched him knock out for the night. I knew the days ahead were going to be difficult.

Afraid to waste all our money on the motel stay, I immediately began searching for a way to have the truck repaired so that we could get back on the road. California was closer than ever, so I didn't want to waste too much time or resources in a place like Cuervo.

The motel manager recommended a nearby garage, which I walked to, three miles in the blistering New Mexico sun.

A slow-talking Texan man agreed to stop by the motel to assess the truck, for a fee, of course. I handed him fifty dollars cash and made the journey back to the motel.

When I got there, Gauge was awake, clumsily attempting to heat up a package of dry noodles on our electric hot plate. My heart sank at his apparent helplessness, but I was sure not to say or do anything that would seem like any form of pity. I knew he would despise that.

"You got that?" I asked, the cool blast of the room's air conditioning welcoming me like an eager puppy.

"Yeah," he mumbled, awkwardly smashing a fork into the tiny sauce pan with his rigid, casted hand.

I could sense his annoyance, but I didn't interfere. Instead, I began combining the bits of hidden cash I had stuffed in various hiding places, so that I could have an exact total of our overall funds.

I felt Gauge eyeing me from the nearby counter where he was struggling to prepare his meal.

"What did you find out?" he asked, keeping his attention on the boiling contents of the pan. "What is it gonna cost to get the truck up and running?"

"I don't know," I sighed, counting and recounting the collection of bills. "The mechanic is going to stop by on his way home and take a look at it."

"For free?" he continued, poking at the hot plate, trying to switch it off.

"I had to give him fifty."

"Shit," he said, giving up on the plate's switch and resorting to awkwardly pulling the plug from the wall.

"We don't have much choice, Gauge," I replied, separating the cash and replacing it to the various hiding spots. "Unless we wanna stay here in New Mexico, we have to do what needs to be done to get back on the road."

I looked over at him, his appearance both comical and arousing. He wore nothing but a pair of white briefs, his collection of casts and bandages accenting his body like snow on a barren oak tree.

"Yeah, I get it," he grumbled, prodding the handle of the saucepan with both hand casts.

"Gauge," I said softly as I approached him, "let me help you."

He looked up at me, his face tired and pathetic. I knew it was killing him to be so helpless, but he agreed to let me at least pour the boiled noodles into a bowl.

I tried not to stare as I watched him fumble and curse as he attempted to move the contents of the plain soup into his mouth. I said nothing until he finally requested my assistance.

"Can you help me with this, babe?" he asked in a childlike tone. "I can't do shit with these casts."

I smiled slightly as I moved toward him, lifting the bowl and twisting a small wad of noodles onto the fork. He closed his eyes as I fed him, his self-sufficiency and dignity forgotten.

I didn't speak until the meal was through, wiping the dribble from his chin and assisting him back beneath the blankets of the bed.

"Thank you, babe," he said quietly as I tucked him in. I kissed his head and went into the bathroom, turning the shower on full blast so that he could not hear me sobbing.

***

THE SUN HAD NEARLY set beyond the endless desert horizon when the mechanic finally knocked on the door. I stood beside him as he tugged and jiggled various wires and tubes in the engine, murmuring to himself as he completed his diagnosis.

"It's a few things," he announced, a toothpick clinging to the corner of his lips. "I can tow it to my shop and have it going in a day or two."

"For how much?" I asked, not interested in being swindled, prepared to firmly negotiate.

"I can have you back on the road for three fifty," he declared, wiping his grease-covered hands on a red rag that hung from one of his pockets.

"You can't cut me a break?" I asked, keeping my eyes gripped on his.

He stared at me, the chewed toothpick bobbing up and down as he contemplated my question.

"I suppose we could work us out a deal," he replied, his Texas drawl accenting each of his words.

"Thanks, man. I really appreciate it," I said, relief lifting from my chest like a flock of birds fleeing a thunderstorm. "We don't have much on us, and we are trying to make it to California."

The man eyed me curiously, following my words toward the motel room door.

"Who's we?" he asked, returning his eyes to mine.

I hesitated, suddenly afraid to have some sort of repeat encounter as at the restaurant, so I quickly chose my response carefully.

"My brother and I," I answered flatly, moving my eyes to the ground so that he would not sense the lie.

"Hmm," he mumbled, licking his lips and adjusting the toothpick.

"I'm thinking you and me could settle this back at the shop," he continued, removing his cap to scratch his balding scalp.

"What do you mean?" I asked, my heart sensing the new tone of the conversation and therefore responding with an accelerated pace.

"I think you know," he answered, winking.

I closed my eyes and shook my head.

"No, mister," I whispered. "No."

Reopening my eyes, I was stunned to see him fondling the crotch area of his dark blue coveralls. I gasped slightly and looked away.

"Come on, boy," he taunted, raising and lowering his brow. "I can tell you are a cocksucker."

"Forget it," I fired back, raising my hands to grip the open truck hood.

"Hey!" he growled, gripping my left wrist with his hand. "You may not have a choice in this."

I stared at him as he carefully scanned the motel parking lot with his beady eyes.

"I am the only mechanic around for miles. If you wanna get back on the road, it looks like you are gonna have to provide the full payment."

He moved his face toward mine.

"Including tip," he whispered into my ear, his breath reeking of chewing tobacco and cigarettes.

He stumbled as I forced his hand from my wrist and slammed the rusted hood shut.

I hesitated a moment before returning to face him.

"I've got a gun in that room," I replied, my voice unwavering and direct, despite my adrenaline-ravaged pulse. "If you don't get the fuck outta here, right now, I won't hesitate to shoot your dick off."

He just looked at me, wide-eyed and suspicious.

"Don't make me say it twice."

I started to make my way toward the room, when an unfamiliar voice broke the silence.

"I think this young man asked you to leave," a deep and powerful baritone reverberated like an unexpected thunderclap.

I turned to see an exceptionally tall Native American man towering over the mechanic.

The mechanic's smirking expression had morphed into a look of fear and shock.

I watched as he tossed one final glance at me before turning in the direction of his truck. Once inside, he fired the engine, revved it several times, threw it into gear, and peeled out of the parking lot. His beady eyes glared at us as he fled.

"Thank you," I stated sincerely, my voice now shaking with the racing of my heart.

"Mind if I look at your engine?" the man queried, his expression firm, yet his eyes gentle and friendly.

"Um, yeah, sure," I swallowed, my throat tense and dry.

I started to shiver as the desert night opened its cloak over the landscape like a soft sheet spreading over a bed.

The man prodded and tinkered, finally lifting his head and gently closing the hood.

"What about your Indian?" he questioned, nodding his head toward the motel room.

"Huh?" I asked, both on purpose and out of genuine surprise.

"I saw you roll it in there yesterday. Perhaps it needs less work than this Chevy."

I could only stare at him, fearful yet intrigued. I was also suspicious of some unspoken intention.

"Um, look," I started, rubbing my hands over my exposed arms in an attempt to warm myself, "I don't have much to pay with. I think that is why that guy was harassing me."

The man smiled at me.

"He was harassing you because he is the sort of man who tries to meet his needs through fear and demand. It has nothing to do with your ability to pay or not."

We stared at each other for what felt like hours.

Finally, I agreed to let him see the Indian, some internal voice assuring me it would be okay.

The man looked around the room as we entered, allowing his eyes to rest on a sleeping Gauge. I closed the door and directed him to where the lifeless bike rested in the corner near the curtained window.

"Here it is," I stated, plopping my hands on the leather seat, attempting to gain his attention.

He continued to stare at Gauge, a soft, paternal-like expression falling over his face. It was as though he had been waiting to see him, his aged and worn demeanor appearing bright and almost youthful as he took in the sight of the sleeping young man. I was cautious yet moved by what I saw.

"Right," he said softly, finally moving his gaze to the bike.

I stood over him as he slowly ran his hands over it, careful and loving, like someone reuniting with a long-lost relative. I swore I could see tears shimmering in his eyes in the faint light of the room as he continued to prudently feel and inspect the Indian. Though I wanted to, I was unable to interrupt him, somehow captive and still as I witnessed the moment.

"I could have this running for you by morning," he stated, calmly raising to his feet.

"How do you know?" I asked, my face churning in wonder and curiosity. "You didn't even try to start it."

The man stared at me before smiling.

"I just know, son," he replied, returning his attention to the motorcycle.

"Um, well, how much do you want?"

He didn't answer. Instead, he turned his head back toward Gauge, the glistening water in his eyes now distinct and obvious. The site took my breath away.

"It won't cost you anything," he answered, keeping his powerful yet tender gaze on Gauge. "I want to help you."

He turned his head to face me, the lines and markings of his skin as scarred and varied as the parched desert floor. It was as though he had materialized from the cracked sand, appearing just in time to intervene with the mechanic.

"Okay," I answered, somehow comfortable and trusting of his offer.

I watched silently as he carefully rolled the Indian from the room. I didn't ask where he was taking it or at what time I could expect him tomorrow. I only stared, absorbing his presence as if hypnotized by a campfire flame.

I closed the door and returned to the bedside, unpacking the suitcase and consolidating it into Gauge's worn-out knapsack.

Then, I slipped beneath the covers beside a softly snoring Gauge, knowing that in the morning we would be leaving behind much of our limited belongings. We would be headed to California, though. Just us and the Indian.

***

I AWOKE TO THE sound of gentle knocking. Scurrying to dress myself, I opened the door and squinted into the blazing sunlight at the face of the man. Behind him was the Indian, glistening in the morning sun like a shiny brass instrument.

I shook my head in disbelief at how clean and polished it appeared. It was almost as if it had been completely rebuilt, each part and facet brand new from the factory assembly line.

"Wow!" I finally managed to speak. "What did you do to it?"

The man smiled, his face brilliant and illuminated by the rising sun.

"Just a bit of tender, loving care," he answered, keeping his eyes on the Indian. "Aside from a few engine fixes, it just needed a good waxing."

"It's incredible!" I exclaimed, inching from the doorway and toward the gleaming bike. "Wait till Gauge sees it!"

"How is he?" the man asked, his voice now concerned and worried. "Gauge?"

I looked up at him as I stood before the Indian, the heat of the sun as it reflected off the freshly polished chrome warming and prickling over my skin like a mother's loving kisses over the soft flesh of her newborn.

"He's recovering," I answered, carefully watching the man's reaction. "He still has a ways to go, but the doctors say he will be fine."

The man looked at me, his gleaming eyes lit by the yellow light blasting off the Indian. He smiled and nodded, content with my response.

I turned my attention back to the bike, still flabbergasted at how beautiful it was. I couldn't wait for Gauge to lay his eyes on it. I knew it would be good for him. He desperately needed something wonderful to happen in his world.

I lifted my head to thank the man, but he was gone. Vanished. I scanned the parking lot with my eyes, even turning to view the street. Nothing. Without a word or even a sound, he had completely disappeared.

A bit unnerved, I made my way back to the room, spooked yet somehow comforted. Gauge was just placing his feet on the floor as I came through the door.

"Gauge!" I exclaimed. "You have to come see the Indian!"

He looked up at me with sleep-weary eyes, his expression dazed and confused.

"Come!" I urged, moving to assist him to the door. "You're not going to believe this!"

He lifted his casts to block the sun as he moved from the darkness of the room and into the blaring light. I watched as his eyes focused on the bike.

"It's like my dream," he said after a long moment, allowing the casts to fall at his side.

I stared at him curiously.

"What dream?" I asked, moving to help him as he shuffled closer to the motorcycle.

"I dreamed last night that my dad came here," he answered, not allowing his eyes to venture from the bike. "I dreamed that he fixed up the Indian for us."

I could only look at him, my words silent behind my rapid blinking.

I watched breathlessly as Gauge caressed the bike with his oversized hand casts. His eyes glittered like two pearls exposed to the sunlight for the very first time, their oyster shell casings cracked and broken on the ocean floor.

"It was a man," I finally mumbled, my voice trapped and pressed by the weight of my emotion. "He was an Indian."

I chuckled, realizing the irony of it all.

"An Indian fixed the Indian."

Gauge looked at me inquisitively, his face bright and soft like a child's. He nodded and smiled before drifting his gaze back to the bike.

I let him be as I returned to the room to finish gathering our things. I pressed and smashed all the clothing I could into the sole pack and disregarded the rest. The sauce pan, the hot plate, it would all have to stay. I slid the straps of the knapsack over my shoulder and walked out of the room, tossing the keys to the truck into the driver's side window as I made my way back to Gauge and the motorcycle.

"Let's go," I announced, strapping the enormous knapsack to the back of the bike. Gauge shook his head rapidly, darting his eyes between the truck and the Indian.

"What do you mean?" he asked, his face twisting in confusion. "What about the rest of our shit? What about the pickup?"

"It's fine," I stated, impressed at how certain and secure my words were. I didn't question a thing. I simply reacted to the soothing sound of my inner voice.

"To California," I said, smiling as I lifted one of the beat-up helmets over my head.

Gauge looked at me nervously as I fastened the strap of the second helmet below his chin. He didn't say a word as he struggled to place himself behind me on the bike.

Wrapping his casted and bandaged arms around my waist, I kick-started the engine, which growled and purred like a dominant male lion addressing his pride, and steadied the bike with my left leg.

Having never maneuvered a motorcycle on my own, I twisted the throttle and transported us into the street. Gauge didn't flinch as we sped onto the highway, the heated wind of the New Mexico sky blasting around us as if exhaled by the gods.

We prowled into the sun-blazed distance, the vision and memory of the Native American man's gentle face smiling at me in my mind. I would never know who he was or even his name, but I would always remember how he selflessly and silently saved us.

As we raced toward the fleeing heatwaves of the infinite horizon, I smiled, the feeling of Gauge pressed against my back the unspoken security I needed as we rumbled into the unknown.

***

WE MADE IT TO the Grand Canyon just as the sun began to set. The golden orb caressed the massive natural wonder, illuminating it like Heaven. No photograph or television program could have ever prepared me for what this majestic place looked like in person. Parking the bike, the heated sigh of the engine exhaling its relief, we stood side by side at the edge of magnificence.

Neither of us spoke as we basked in the excellence. I felt a sense of humbled meekness and boyish pride at the idea of being a child of the God who created this splendor.

After the sun had long descended below the western edge of the endless canyon, we rolled the bike toward a patch of trees, careful not to signal our presence to the patrolling park rangers.

I fed Gauge one of the two plain bologna sandwiches we had picked up at a gas station along the way. I watched as he washed it down with a swig of the water fountain water I had filled our canteen with.

Placing a collection of shirts, jeans, and motel towels into a makeshift bed, I wrapped Gauge in our sole blanket and inched myself beside him.

The heat of the Indian's engine began to fade as the dampness of the night introduced its chill. I pressed myself into Gauge, allowing my breath to warm the side of his neck.

There was no shame or embarrassment when I released the contents of my bladder between us. Gauge moaned in his sleep, the warm glide of the urine seeping beneath his hips and upper legs.

I floated in a suspension of lucid dreams and consciousness. The rhythmic chatter of my teeth lulled my senses as they fired their relentless warning cries of hypothermia to my brain.

Just as the iceless kiss of the night became unbearable, the sun returned, peeking its heated brilliance above the treetops like a wingless angel.

I woke Gauge and helped him into fresh clothing. We boarded the Indian and continued on our way, the magnetic pull of the canyon shadowing us for miles.

Sometime around noon, Gauge began to heat up. I assumed it was from the unforgiving glare of the desert sun, but soon discovered that an unseen inferno raged inside him.

I diverted our westbound travels a bit north toward Las Vegas, the voice within me assuring that it was the right choice. Once inside the city limits, I was blind to the colorful sights and sounds that echoed around us like a neon spacecraft. Instead, I obediently followed the road signs to the nearest hospital.

Gauge was nearly unresponsive as we rumbled into the parking lot. I pulled the Indian directly next to the emergency room doors, uncaring as to any issue it would cause.

A white-haired nurse ran to fetch a wheelchair the minute she laid eyes on Gauge. She pulled me aside as a team of medics whisked him beyond the giant swinging doors that separated the waiting area from the rest of the medical tower. I was pulled into a small conference room.

"Please fill these out thoroughly," the nurse commanded, her eyes scanning over me as she placed a large clipboard on the desk before me.

"Do you need to see a doctor as well?" she asked, tipping her head in concern.

"No," I answered hoarsely, my throat tight and severely parched. "I just need some water."

"Of course," the nurse replied, her eyes unmoving as she exited the room.

I completed the forms to the best of my ability and returned them to where the white-haired woman resided behind a seemingly boundless nurse's station. She flipped through the documents, her lips pursed as she briefed over each page.

"Insurance?" she asked, keeping her eyes on the scribbled information I had provided.

"No," I replied, my voice tired and broken.

She peered up at me, her bird-like stare zigzagging over my face as though she could see beneath my skin and directly into my thoughts.

"I see," she continued, returning her focus to the clipboard.

"How do you intend to pay for Mr. Paulson's services today?" she asked, the reference to Gauge by his last name a bit striking and foreign to me.

"I am not sure," I said, lowering my head in embarrassment.

I could feel her eyes dart over me again as I stood before her in shame. Finally, she reached for another dozen forms and stapled them together.

"Fill these out," she directed, shoving the new tome at my fingertips. "These will guide you through the Federal Assistance Program."

I looked up at her, my stare burdened with hunger, relief, and exhaustion.

"How about we take you back to see a doctor first," she suggested after I failed to reply.

"No. I'm fine. Really."

She continued to assess me with her jumpy stare.

"Very well," she sighed, sliding a pen over the paper stack.

I was grateful when she later provided me several packs of plain, saltless crackers. I gobbled them down like a hungry duckling at a park pondside. She eyed me cautiously before returning to the desk.

Nearly an hour or so later, one of the orderlies located me.

"Are you here with Gauge Paulson?" he asked, his dark blue medical scrubs crinkled and covered with various lint and debris.

"Yes," I answered, my voice still weighted and broken by the burning of my throat.

"First off, we had to move your motorcycle."

My heart jumped as I looked toward the mammoth glass doors.

"No worries, I had security place it in a storage shed. No one will disturb it there."

I closed my eyes in relief, the rushing exhale of my lungs escaping through me like a desert dirt devil.

"Second, Mr. Paulson is going to have to stay the night," he declared, pulling a small piece of paper from one of his oversized scrub pockets.

"Here is the number to a shelter if you need a place to go."

I looked up at him as he placed the paper into my palm.

"Wait, what?"

My words fell between us like hail in a rainstorm.

"Sir, I assume this by the state of your appearance," he continued. "There is no judgment. I am simply providing a civil service."

I could only stare at him. The suggestion that I was homeless was both baffling and offensive to comprehend.

"If needed, of course," he concluded when I didn't respond with words.

"I'm fine, thank you," I grumbled, crushing the paper in my fist.

The orderly stared at me, his brown eyes reflecting my physically and emotionally drained face.

"Very well," he said, turning to go.

"Wait!" I called. "What about Gauge? How is he? When can I see him?"

"He has an infection," he stated, turning back to face me. "Those casts should have been changed a week ago. Had you not brought him in today, I can't promise that he would have remained alive much longer."

His words fell over me like an acid rain, each syllable searing into my flesh.

"What? Are you serious?"

"Yes, son. All sorts of bacteria and crazy things start to fester when casts aren't maintained or changed properly. Your friend here looks like he's worn his through the Amazon and back."

I couldn't speak, my voice paralyzed in disbelief.

"Anyhow, I take it you are not related to him," the man stated, almost accusatorily.

My mind raced for a response, but something inside delivered one before I could approve of it.

"I'm his boyfriend," I heard my voice state, assured and certain.

The orderly nodded, a slight smile moving over his previously expressionless face.

"That's what I assumed," he said. "It's okay. Give me ten minutes and I will get you to him."

He leaned forward and whispered, "I'm gay too, so I am going to bend a bit of rules for some of my brethren."

He patted my knee and returned to his full height. Confusion and relief circled over my face like a living collage. That same inner voice I had been hearing so clearly the past few days issued a mental and emotional reprieve.

I watched as the orderly disappeared behind the palace-sized ivory doors, leaving me alone to sit with my worry and exhaustion.

I jumped when he later tapped my shoulder, placing a finger to his lips to signify my silent obedience.

I mimicked his steps as we slipped past the swinging doors and into the internal twists and turns of the emergency room.

We stopped before a closed curtain, the sound of whirring machinery beeping and clicking behind it.

The orderly parted a corner of the fabric, motioning for me to tuck between it.

I gasped when I saw Gauge, his face sunken, his nose and mouth covered by a tangle of various tubing and hoses.

"Don't worry," the orderly eased, placing a hand on my shoulder. "It looks worse than it is. We gave him some medication, so he's just sleeping. He will be good as new once we get that infection out of him."

A tear fell from my cheek and onto the bedside, its liquid presence dancing and dazzling from the light of the nearby glowing machinery.

"So," the orderly whispered, "time to tell the truth. Where are you staying?"

I closed my eyes and shook my head, the truth of our circumstances snapping my gathering tears like a needle pricking the skin of a water balloon. Instantly, a gush of water began glazing over my skin like liquid molasses atop a Christmas ham. I felt helpless and stupid as I stood alone before an unconscious Gauge and an inquisitive stranger.

"Shh," the man cooed. "Listen, everything is going to be okay. I promise you."

I turned my head to face him, the wavering of my fleeing tears distorting my vision.

"I get off in about fifty minutes," he continued. "We can talk about everything then."

I squinted as his face came into view, his brown eyes soft and sympathetic, his brow creased with concern, his lips attempting a reassuring smile.

"Okay?" he asked when my words again failed me.

I nodded, moving my hands to wipe away the silent flooding of my skin.

He sat me in a nearby chair, patted my shoulder, and slipped behind the curtain.

I watched in a mental tsunami of fear and worry as Gauge's chest lifted and fell in unison with the breathing and ticking of the collection of electronics. I wasn't sure how much time had passed when the orderly appeared again, this time donning a pair of light blue jeans and a brown corduroy jacket.

He squatted beside me, placing both of his hands over mine.

"I'd like for you to come home with me," he whispered gently, allowing his expression to accent the certainty of his words.

I fixed my eyes on his suspiciously, concern and doubt marching over my expression as if displayed on the letterbox screens of Times Square.

"I get it," he said smiling, nodding his head in understanding. "It's wise to be cautious. But I give you my word that this is safe. It's a solid offer."

The silent voice within responded by lifting me from the chair and nodding my head. I took one last look at Gauge, kissed him on the forehead, and then followed the man beyond the curtain.

***

HIS NAME WAS PAUL Morales, a twenty-seven-year-old medical student from Arizona. He was interning at the hospital, cramming in a seemingly endless cycle of classes and labs in between the hours he kept as an orderly and those he spent asleep.

His tiny one-bedroom apartment was charming. There was a large glass sliding door that overlooked the street, various replicas of famous paintings adorning the walls, and a massive spool that had been sanded and varnished to look like some form of high-quality wood.

"You can take my bed, and I will crash on the couch," Paul announced as we entered the tiny living space. "Please don't try and decline out of politeness. I insist you have the bed."

I smiled when he turned to check my reaction to his decree. I really didn't care where I slept, but I was grateful that it would be in an actual dwelling with a traditional bed, a definite improvement from the truck cabin, the desert floor, or the makeshift pile of towels and T-shirts I had been finding slumber on the past several days.

"I head back to the hospital around 5:00 a.m., so I will wake you around 4:30 so that you can get ready."

I nodded, feeling the weight of my exhaustion slowly creeping over my entire body like the shadow of the setting sun over the street below the sliding glass door.

"Do you like Chinese food?" he asked, tossing his pile of bags, books, and various articles of clothing onto the corner of an under-stuffed, worn-out hunter green couch.

"Um, yeah, that's fine," I replied, the extent of my stress, fear, and worry accenting each of my words.

Paul stared at me, his eyes methodically shifting between mine.

"You really love him, don't you?" he asked, his inquisitive stare unbroken.

Unexpectedly, the relentless spinning of emotion seeped over my eyes and down my face. I struggled to breathe under the sudden and powerful surge of the water.

"Aw, man," Paul said softly, moving forward to embrace me. "Let it out, dude."

I couldn't speak for at least five minutes. I could only cry, focus on breathing, and then cry some more.

When my tears finally dried, the lingering droplets that dangled along the edges of my lids shimmered in the light like dewdrops under the moon. I sat on the couch, allowing the remainder of the outpour to flow through me in one long, enormous sigh.

"Feel better?" Paul asked, locating a tissue box on the small table that stood between the wall and the couch.

"Thanks," I sniffed, pulling several tissues from the box.

"It's a beautiful thing, you know," Paul stated, placing the tissue box between us. "What you have with Gauge. It's a mighty thing."

He paused, waiting for me to meet his gaze.

"Never take that for granted. Many people go their whole lives never finding a fraction of what I can see in the two of you."

I smiled, lowering my head back to my chest, watching my fingers as they nervously twisted and fumbled the collection of tissues in my grasp.

"Where did you meet?"

We spent the next hour or so chatting about Gauge and me, my family, and the journey we had taken since leaving

South Florida. Paul never interrupted. Instead, he listened intently, keeping his eyes directly in line with mine. His interest appeared authentic, which was both comforting and a bit unnerving.

"So have you spoken to your folks since you left?" he asked, rising from the couch and moving toward the kitchen.

"No," I replied, keeping my eyes attached to the twisting tissues, which had now been obliterated to a cycling collection of shredded bits.

"You need to call them," Paul directed, returning to the couch with two bottles of beer.

"I don't know," I answered, watching the remaining shreds of tissue disintegrate into the rest of the pile.

"Hey," Paul spoke loudly, placing one of the ice-cold bottles into my hand. "They are your parents, dude. You need to at least let them know that you are okay."

I discarded the annihilated tissue bits onto the giant varnished wooden spool and twisted the bottle cap.

"Of course I've thought about it," I said, chugging a large mouthful of the fizzy golden liquid.

"Then do it. Now."

I pulled the bottle from my lips, nearly choking from the surprise of his sudden command.

"It's long distance, but I don't care," he declared, leaning toward the side table to retrieve a cream-colored telephone. "This is worth the extra cost on my bill."

He plopped the phone onto my lap, the chime of the bell echoing with the impact. I looked up at Paul, confusion and worry appearing over my bloodshot, liquefied stare.

"Go on, Dustin," he commanded. "I am not ordering the food or allowing us to go to bed until you speak to one, or both, of your parents."

For some reason, be it the slowly churning alcohol within my veins or the surrender of my resistance to the suffocation of my exhaustion, I obeyed him, without argument or even a slight hesitation. Before I could process what was happening, I was on the phone with my father.

"Hello?" I heard him say, the familiarity and recognition of his voice warming over me faster than the carbonated pool inside my stomach.

"Dad?" I choked, my throat still burning from the outpour of my tears and the bubbled assault of the beer.

Silence.

"Dustin?" he whispered, his voice cracking. "Dustin, is that you?"

My tears returned, this time sliding down my skin softly and slowly, as though healing over the salt-tinged irritation left behind by the first wave of emotion.

"Yes, Dad."

Paul left the room as the conversation with my father began to progress. In ten minutes, I learned that he knew everything, the details of my attack at the bathhouse, the encounters with my mother, even the fact that I had been in Tennessee for six months. Apparently, a few weeks after I left, Detective Sherman finally fulfilled his promise to contact my parents. The assailant had been arrested, identified by the faceless presence behind the rainbow-colored ticket window. When my parents failed to provide my whereabouts, my mother broke down and came clean about everything, even admitting to the violent assault at Aunt Mert's. Detective Sherman made a few phone calls, and within a month an investigator had traced me to Tennessee. My parents declined the detective's offer to confront me. Instead, they accepted my leaving and found comfort and peace of mind in knowing I was safe with Gauge.

"Where's Mom?" I finally asked after my father began babbling about pointless details of his job.

"She's at Bible study," my father answered after a slow yet burdened sigh. "She goes all the time. She's very involved with the church now. I hardly see her."

"Please tell her that I'm okay, Dad," I said, my slow-falling tears quickening their pace. "Tell her I love her…and that I forgive her."

I could hear my father sobbing, his voice broken by the enormity of his emotion.

"I will, Son," he finally answered, his words heavy with sorrow and regret.

"And, Son," he continued. "I want you to know that I love you. I always will. Your mother was wrong about me."

I listened as he struggled to tame his tear-exhausted breathing.

"I don't care that you are gay," he said, his voice suddenly calm and controlled. "You are my son, and I will always love you. No matter what."

The force of my tears slid the phone from my ear and onto my lap. A tireless cyclone of relief and sadness funneled around me as I struggled to regain my composure. I looked up tosee Paul smiling at me from the doorway of his bedroom.

"I love you too, Dad. So much."

We ended the call with the promise that I would contact them again in a week's time. He thanked me for calling and assured me that he would relay my message of love and forgiveness to my mother once she arrived home. I closed my eyes and wept, the remainder of my body's surplus of water for tears drying, leaving me with only the convulsing heave of a tearless sob.

Paul returned to the couch, wrapping his arms around me until my breathing slowed and I was able to speak.

"See," he said, smiling as our eyes met. "This is exactly what you needed, my friend."

I nodded in agreement, thanking him with a slobbered, snotty embrace.

He patted my shoulder triumphantly and playfully messed up my hair. Taking the phone from my lap, he declared, "Now, let's order up that Chinese!"

***

GAUGE WAS AWAKE WHEN we arrived at the hospital the next morning. His dark eyes dazzled under the fluorescents when he saw me. As if separated for years, we embraced in silence, the beating of our hearts speaking the words we could not say.

"Where did you go?" he whispered, holding me in his arms.

"One of the orderlies who was taking care of you last night let me stay at his place," I replied, running my fingers through his thick, dark hair.

"I missed you," he cooed, his voice tender and soft like a child's.

"I missed you too, baby."

Paul entered from behind the curtain.

"Looks like they are letting you outta here tonight, my man," he announced, holding up a clipboard full of charts.

"What about the infection?" I asked, allowing Gauge to pull from our embrace so that he could sit up straight in the bed.

"The doctors seem to think it has cleared enough to where he will be fine going home with some antibiotics."

Gauge and I stared at Paul, both relieved yet bewildered by the unexpected news.

"Well, hell, boys, one of you show some sort of excitement! This is an amazing improvement!"

Gauge and I faced each other and kissed. I looked down at his arms, admiring the new collection of clean and simplified casts and bandages.

"Doctor is gonna want you in physical therapy," Paul continued, leaning to read one of the machine screens. "Lucky for you, that is what I am going to school for."

He smiled, moving the clipboard behind his back and standing tall like a soldier saluting a flag.

"What does that mean?" I asked, pulling a nearby chair closer to the bedside.

"That means," Paul started, sliding the clipboard into a wooden slot on the end of the bed, "that I can provide the service for free."

I looked at Gauge, who was listening intently to Paul.

"Without insurance, there is no way you guys would be able to foot the bill on PT. I could bring Gauge with me to my practical lab, and we could work his hands."

Gauge turned his head to me, a look of confusion and uncertainty floating over his face.

"Wow," I said, appreciative yet surprised by the offer. "I don't know what to say, Paul."

I kept my eyes on Gauge's, nodding and smiling my approval for him to see.

"Hey, I should be thanking you!" Paul exclaimed, placing his hand over Gauge's blanketed ankle. "I am in desperate need of more lab hours, and working with Gauge on a consistent basis will certainly get me some."

I watched as Gauge stared at Paul a long moment, a look of distrust and suspicion locking his expression. Sensing the sudden and unspoken tension, Paul released his hand from Gauge's leg and retreated to the corner near the curtain.

"Well," he said, clearing his throat as if attempting to clear the energy of the space around us. "Let me know if that would work for you. You both are more than welcome to stay with me during the therapy. As long as it takes. I would be more than happy to host you."

I smiled before returning my attention to Gauge, who remained staring and silent in the hospital bed.

I looked back at Paul, who curiously returned Gauge's stare. The tension in the room snaked around the three of us as powerful and tight as a python constricting its prey. No one spoke for what felt like hours.

"That would be great!" I finally responded, lifting from the chair, reclaiming my stance next to Gauge.

I felt Gauge place one of his casted hands over my wrist where it rested on top of his upper leg.

"Awesome," Paul replied, flashing a massive grin before disappearing behind the curtain.

Gauge turned to me the second Paul was gone.

"Why are you accepting this guy's offer?" he asked, his confusion and concern transforming into suspicion and frustration. "He's up to something. I can tell. He obviously wants something from us."

"Gauge, no," I said, attempting to reassure him with the certainty of my voice, but for some reason, it was lacking. "He is a good guy, I swear. He was so kind to me last night. He even had me call my dad."

Gauge looked at me, his worried expression melting into one of shock and interest.

"Really?" he replied, scooting himself higher against the stack of pillows he reclined against. "What happened?"

I spent the next ten minutes detailing the conversation with my father. Gauge listened intently, his eyes wide, his mouth slightly agape from his bated breath.

"Wow, babe," he said smiling when I concluded. "Come here. I'm so happy for you."

He closed his casted hands around me, squeezing me tight in his embrace. I pressed my face into his hair, slowly absorbing the comforting smell of his scalp with my nose. I couldn't wait to finally lie beside him again, falling asleep with his gentle heartbeat thumping next to mine in a rhythmic lullaby.

"So, are you sure we can trust this guy?" he asked after a long silence, our arms still entwined.

"I think so," I answered, pulling away so that I could see his face. "He was very generous with me, babe. I really think he just wants to help us."

Gauge stared at me, the twisting of his thoughts spiraling around his pupils like renegade clock cogs.

"Okay," he said after a long, thoughtful pause. "If you say we can trust him, then I will trust him."

I smiled, wrapping my arms around his head in a playful embrace.

We spent the next several hours chitchatting aimlessly and flipping through the limited channels on the ancient television set that hung in the corner of the room. Just after lunch, the doctor finally came around to complete a final check on Gauge.

"Those casts of yours need to come off in another two weeks," the doctor announced, rapidly scribbling over Gauge's charts like a toddler just discovering an ink pen. "I was told that you will be seeing a private physical therapist afterward?"

Gauge looked at me before turning to answer the doctor. It was as though he were allowing me one final chance to dissuade the agreement with Paul. I gently smiled and nodded my approval.

"That's correct," Gauge replied, watching as the doctor carefully examined his casts.

"Be sure and follow through with the entire course of therapy," the doctor ordered, peering down at Gauge with an authoritative glance. "From the X-rays, you suffered some serious fractures and perhaps some nerve damage. The only way to ensure the best chance of a full recovery is to work those hands the moment the casts come off."

Gauge nodded obediently, a semi-smile cracking over his dried lips.

"Very well. I will send someone in here to discharge you soon. Take care, Mr. Paulson. I wish you a very speedy recovery."

I looked at Gauge, a palpable nervousness filling the room. I could tell he was worried about his hands. Anything less than a full recovery would be a tremendous loss for him. Everything he excelled at, mechanics, cooking, art, it all involved the smooth fluidity of his hands. I knew he was terrified of not regaining that.

Once discharged, Paul led us to the small storage shed where the Indian was stowed. He handed me a key to his apartment, with the promise that he would meet us there later that night after his shift. Gauge eyed the transaction suspiciously but said nothing as we boarded the bike.

Kick-starting the familiar growl of the engine to life, we pulled out of the hospital parking lot and into the Las Vegas traffic. I could feel Gauge behind me, moving his head in every direction as we sputtered in complete sensory overload down the Strip.

Arriving at Paul's apartment building, I parked the Indian next to a street lamp and assisted Gauge as he disembarked.

"Paul said there was a chain in his closet we can use," I stated, unstrapping the giant knapsack from the back of the bike.

"Of course he has a chain," Gauge murmured cattily as I unclasped his helmet's chin strap.

"What does that mean?" I asked, collecting both helmets and the knapsack into my overloaded arms.

"Nothing, nothing," he replied, shaking his head at his own words. "Let's just chain the bike and get inside. You go get the chain from the freak's bedroom, and I'll wait here."

I shot him an annoyed yet understanding glare before obeying his command.

Once inside the apartment, I unloaded the weighty baggage and drifted into Paul's bedroom. Locating the closet, I slid one of the large paneled doors open and started in amazement.

There, amongst his tennis shoes and school books, was a vast array of leatherwear, masks, handcuffs, chains, and whips. The sight was so overwhelming that it took my brain several long moments to compute and process what it was seeing. I laughed to myself as I realized that Gauge's catty accusation regarding the chain was correct. Shuffling through the impressive collection, I located an actual bicycle chain and lock. I slid the door shut and bounded out of the apartment and back to Gauge, who eyed me suspiciously the moment he spotted my smiling face.

"You were right," I confessed, pausing before him with the chain proudly displayed in my hands.

"About what?"

"Our friend Paul is a bit of a freak," I confirmed, squatting down to snake the chain through the spokes of the Indian's front tire.

"What do you mean?" Gauge continued his inquiry, his face pinched in utter confusion.

"Whips, chains, masks, leather. You name it, he's got it."

I wrapped the remaining bit of chain around the streetlamp and clamped the large lock. I looked up at Gauge, who shook his head disapprovingly.

"Dustin, no," he said, his face less amused and far more concerned. "I seriously have a bad feeling about this guy."

"Oh, come on, Gauge," I retorted, raising to my full height. "We can't judge this guy based on his sex toy collection."

"It has nothing to do with that, Dustin. I just have a bad feeling about him. I don't know why. I just do."

I stared at him a moment, somehow comprehending the silence of his fear before brushing it off altogether.

"We don't have much choice, Gauge," I said, wrapping my arm with his. "He is giving us a place to stay, and he is going to work with you on your hands. You heard what the doctor said today. You know how important it is that you get this physical therapy."

I looked at his face as we slowly ascended the stairway to Paul's second-floor apartment. I could see that he was listening.

"How else could we afford to get you physical therapy? This guy is doing us a major favor by doing it for free."

Gauge didn't respond as we entered the apartment. He looked around, took in the limited detail of the space, and then sighed.

"Yeah, I know," he replied, the sound of exhaustion and defeat trailing his words. "Still, there's something about all this that just doesn't sit right with me."

"Yeah, yeah. For now, Colombo, let's just clean you up and get you into bed."

We didn't speak as I helped him undress and climb into Paul's full-sized bed, the springs revealing their wear with an audible display of squeaks, pops, and groans.

Kissing Gauge on the lips, I exited the room and returned to the living area to situate our belongings. I didn't attempt to distract myself as curious thoughts surrounding Paul pranced around my head like a mischievous kitten.

As I neatly organized our pack and tidied up the small kitchen and living space, something inside me agreed with Gauge's suspicions. Despite the outward kindness and generosity of Paul, there was an air of unease about the apartment I had not sensed the night before. There was something sinister lurking in the shadows of this humble home, and as I crawled into the bed beside a sleeping Gauge, I drifted off with an implicit knowing that we would soon discover what it was.

∗∗∗

THREE WEEKS LATER, GAUGE was finally cast-free. Five days a week, he joined Paul at his practical lab, diligently following through with the physical therapy with zest and discipline. When he wasn't at the lab with Paul, he was home squeezing his multicolored set of rubber therapy balls, twisting a silicone hose, and practicing holding a pen. The pen holding became his staple. He would sit for hours doodling, scribbling, sketching, and writing. Curiosity finally got the best of me, so I flipped through his notebook one day while he was in the shower. I discovered countless letters written to Aunt Mert. He detailed every single facet of our experience since leaving home, providing a nearly weekly account of each and every occurrence and event. I was amazed at the quality and accuracy of the information. He recaptured everything, as if providing a frozen snapshot from his memory. I never realized he paid such close attention to detail, even the most minute and irrelevant information. Finally, one day, I admitted to seeing the letters and asked him about them.

"I saw your letters to Aunt Mert," I casually admitted, busily constructing a twin set of turkey sandwiches. "Are you planning to send them?"

"Maybe," Gauge replied, rotating a pair of therapy balls around in his hands.

"They're really good," I continued, avoiding eye contact as I completed my basic culinary task. "I think you should send them. When was the last time you spoke to her?"

"I called when we first got to Tennessee. I promised her I would, so that's what I did."

"And that was it?" I asked, placing a sandwich before him on the wooden spool.

"Pretty much," he concluded, dropping the rubber balls and carefully grasping the sandwich.

"I wonder if she ever speaks to my parents," I questioned aloud, more to myself than to Gauge.

"Doubt it," Gauge replied, his mouth stuffed full with a chunk of sandwich. "She thinks your mom is a nut job. Aunt Mert ain't about all that drama."

I sat beside him, poking my sandwich with my finger.

"You should probably call her again. Or send the letters. I think she would like to hear from you."

Gauge continued to chew, allowing his eyes to trail toward the sun-blazed sliding glass door.

"She knows I'm okay," he finally replied. "I'll send the letters eventually."

I took a bite of my sandwich, mentally recalling my return phone call to my parents. As promised, I phoned again, and once more my mother was not home but at another Bible study meeting. My father told me she only nodded when he told her of the first conversation and of my message of love and forgiveness. I was hurt and disappointed that she had no verbal response, no return sentiments, or no reply of love.

I didn't plan to call again. I gave my father the telephone number to Paul's apartment. I figured if my mother wanted to reach me, she would. I was home most days, and though I never really kept the thought at the forefront of my mind, I did secretly hope she would call.

I struggled to find work in Las Vegas. I applied to several hotels for housekeeping positions, a few restaurants for server or even busboy spots, but nothing ever came of it.

Paul was hardly home, but when he was, he made the most of our time together by preparing some of the delicious Mexican-inspired dishes his grandmother used to make for him. Gauge interacted with Paul the way two estranged family members would converse under the pressure and awkwardness of a family reunion. Their conversations were light and cordial. I could only assume that it was pretty much the same during their hour-long therapy sessions down at Paul's university.

"We need to think about getting outta here," Gauge stated, his eyes still lingering over the sunny street view beyond the sliding glass. "I've got about another week of therapy, so we should be good to go. How much money do we have?"

I swallowed the mouthful of turkey sandwich, confused and surprised at the sudden mention of the topic.

"Around five hundred dollars," I answered, nervously fidgeting the sandwich in my hands.

"That can get us to California," Gauge replied, turning his head to face me. "We're close now."

I smiled and nodded, suddenly doubtful and uncertain as to the truth of his statement. For some reason, I could not foresee us leaving Nevada. At least, not anytime soon. Something inside me proposed a sense of unease and insecurity, the plan and dream of California now a nearly forgotten distraction.

"Aw, did I miss lunch?" a voice broke the silence. "Damn!"

Gauge and I turned to see Paul entering the room, several overstuffed brown paper grocery bags filling his arms.

I moved to assist him.

"Thank you, my friend," Paul said as I relieved some of his burden.

"What's all this for?" I asked, peering and poking over the tops of the bags.

"Tonight," Paul announced, "is a special night."

Gauge and I stared at him, a look of boredom and disinterest frowning over Gauge's expression.

"I'm having some friends over for dinner," Paul continued, feverishly unloading one of the bag's contents into the refrigerator. "I am hoping the two of you will join us."

I looked over at Gauge, who only stared at me, his expression clear in its disapproval and frustration.

"Sure," I responded, nodding at Gauge in defiance.

"Be nice," I mouthed, watching him roll his eyes in reply.

"Perfect. Dinner will be served around seven."

Paul smiled, his eyes gleaming with a mischievous glint. My heart fluttered in response, a curious yet suspicious feeling seeping over my skin like a rare desert rainstorm.

I returned to Gauge on the couch. He stared straight ahead, sighing, signaling his annoyance with the entire situation.

"Why do we have to do this?" he asked an hour later as we stood in the shower together. "I deal with this guy enough. I don't want to have dinner with him and his friends."

"Gauge," I replied, my voice stern and annoyed, "it is the very least we can do. Paul has been completely hospitable to us. Feeding us, allowing us to stay here, doing your therapy. And all for free. I'm pretty sure the right thing to do is to have dinner with him and his friends when he asks."

Gauge sighed, closing his eyes as he backed his head under the hot stream of the shower water.

I smirked, watching in an aroused silence as the water trickled over his face and down his naked body. The past several nights had been filled with repeated lovemaking. We had gone weeks without so much as touching each other due to Gauge's injuries and subsequent infection. Squeezing and groping every area of my body had quickly become one of his favorite forms of physical therapy. He was certainly out to prove that his hands were back in full commission, at least when it came to intimacy.

I moved toward him, wrapping my arms around him in the water. He returned the embrace, the heated tinge of the shower's torrent enveloping us like a warm, liquid cocoon.

***

THE FIRST OF PAUL's friends began to arrive just before seven o'clock. Each provided a contribution to the dinner, be it a food dish, some form of liquor, or even a dessert.

I smiled and warmly greeted each visitor as they made their way into the living space. Gauge was polite but certainly uninterested in conversing with any of them.

Paul announced that dinner was ready around seven-thirty. The dozen or so guests slowly migrated to the table in response. I had often wondered why Paul had such a large dining room table. It could easily sit ten or more people and dominated the tiny dining area like a bolder in a mud puddle.

From the natural flow of the ongoing conversations, it was clear that these men knew one other. Each appeared to be gay, but none presented themselves as a couple. Each man looked to be solo and familiar with the others. One thing was for certain, every guest was carefully curious and interested in Gauge and me. Several times already, I found myself meeting the shameless and inquisitive stare of one of the men. There was an uneasy energy in the room, at least to me. It felt as though Gauge and I were as much of an interest to each of the guests as the promised dinner meal.

"First," Paul announced, standing at the head of the table with a wine glass in his hand, "I would like to propose a toast."

In unison, the various conversations ceased, and everyone turned their attention to Paul, holding up their own wine glass in response to his proposal.

"I have been blessed and honored to have two very kind, warm, and wonderful gentlemen staying with me for the past month. Both men exude such great love for the other, and I am constantly humbled and amazed to bear witness to their beautiful union. I can only hope and pray that the same blessing will someday be bestowed upon all of us."

The eyes of the entire table turned toward us, the only two people without a glass of wine.

"Cheers!" the group chanted as a chorus.

I smiled nervously, and Gauge looked away. I could tell he was ready to crawl under the table from embarrassment.

"Oh dear," Paul exclaimed. "I completely forgot your wine!"

He moved to the kitchen, returning with two half-filled cylindrical glasses.

"Cheers," he said smiling, clanking his half-empty glass against each of ours.

I smiled and lifted the wineglass to my lips. I looked over at Gauge, who continued to stare at the floor. I allowed a giant mouthful of the warm red wine to slide down my throat before replacing the glass onto the table. I tapped Gauge with my knee, silently urging him to follow my lead, but he ignored me. He never touched his wineglass for the entire dinner.

After the meal, the group gathered in the living room, hovering around the massive wooden spool like eager schoolchildren on the first day of class. Gauge went into the bedroom and closed the door.

Paul presented a board game to the group, watching me as I followed Gauge.

"I don't want to go back out there," Gauge declared as I entered the room. "I did what I agreed to. I ate with them. But I'm done. I don't want to be a part of this anymore."

"A part of what, Gauge?" I asked, my voice filling with disappointment and slight anger.

"This gay shit," he responded, nodding his head toward the living room.

"What the fuck, Gauge?" I scolded, snatching a wet towel from the corner of the bed and tossing it into the open bathroom door. "So having dinner with some people is now considered 'gay shit'?"

I mocked him with a mimicked expression and voice. He eyed me, obviously annoyed, and then slid his body deeper beneath the bedspread.

"Whatever, Gauge," I said, angrily storming back to the door. "Just stay in here and be an asshole. I don't want you out there acting like this anyway."

He didn't respond or even look at me. Instead, he adjusted himself against the pillow and rolled over.

I exited the room, forcefully closing the door behind me. The group looked up as I reentered the living area.

"Everything okay?" Paul asked as I took my place beside him at the spool.

"Yeah," I responded, annoyance and anger still flooding my voice. "He's not playing. He's already in bed."

Paul gazed at me a moment, his eyes lifting to the bedroom door, and then back to me.

"Must have been the wine," he said, smiling.

"Yeah," I laughed, knowing full well that Gauge never touched his glass. "Must be."

I could hardly keep my eyes open as the night progressed. Soon, the game board and pieces began to swirl around in my vision, the peering and staring faces of the men joining in as some hypnotic haze. Slowly, I felt myself begin to lean against Paul. He patted my head as I fell into a very deep sleep.

***

I OPENED MY EYES, the blurry scene of the room a multicolored fuzz. My skin was cold. I lifted one of my arms, its weight heavier than I could ever remember it being, and placed it over my stomach. My skin was bare. Where was I? Where was my shirt?

Slowly, I slid my hand further down, my fingertips running through the coarse tangle of my pubic hair. I was naked.

"He's awake," I heard a voice say, the unclear pillars of color moving around me like fish beneath a rain-disturbed lake.

Suddenly, one of the faces leaned toward me, its presence just close enough for me to make out the detail. It was Paul. I recognized his eyes, though his face was covered by some sort of mask. Then, as if someone turned on a light, I began to see more clearly. The moving figures focused into a wall of bodies, all of them naked and facing me.

***

I DROPPED MY ARM beside me, the familiar roughness of the wooden spool running under my touch.

I mumbled, trying to speak, but it felt as though my face was covered in a thick glaze. My voice was weighted, my speech slurred, as if I were attempting to speak through glue.

"Shit," Paul said, returning to the group. "He must not have drank enough."

I rolled my head from side to side, taking in the sight of the different skin tones of the seemingly endless sea of naked male bodies. A slow-moving wave of terror oozed over me as heavy as the presence that overwhelmed my face and head. I couldn't speak. I could hardly move. I attempted to raise my head, but my body did not respond to my brain's command. Instead, I lay helpless, every limb of my body paralyzed to my repeated mental attempts to move them.

"What do we do?" a voice asked, the bodies shuffling closer. In my dizzy haze, the vision of a variety of penises, some dangling above me, some erect and throbbing, filled my clouded view. The alarming echo of pure fear that soaked around me began to quicken and intensify its pace and calling. I wasn't sure if I was awake or dreaming. All I knew was that I could not move, though every bit of my willpower was shouting for me to raise up or scream.

"Do you still have the syringe?" another voice questioned.

I began to see more clearly, the naked bodies disguising their faces behind an array of masks. My heart began to pound so loudly in my ears that I could no longer hear the voices. Instead, I felt the presence of cold hands and fingertips gliding over my exposed flesh like ants scurrying over a picnic basket.

"Here," one of the voices said as someone lifted my head from the spool. "I'll open his mouth."

In the haze, I could see the bodies parting, a semi-clear visual of Paul coming into view as he neared me, the glistening needle of a syringe rising from his hand.

The surge of panic and fear that clouded around me like a suffocating fog began to lift as something inside me started to bellow and scream. It was several seconds before I realized that the sound was now echoing around me, reverberating around the room like a panther falling victim to a steel trap.

I felt myself being lowered back onto the spool as another voice broke into the sphere of warbled sound.

I felt someone fall onto me, the voice screaming expletives at the room around them. It was Gauge. I could smell his skin beneath his T-shirt and feel the familiar vibration of his deep and powerful voice as it boomed through his chest.

"We didn't touch him!" a voice called out, the wall of bodies retreating into the distance.

Gauge placed his hands around my face, pulling me toward him.

"It's okay, baby, I'm here," he said, his face smashed against mine. "Did they touch you? Are you hurt?"

I shook my head, my voice still locked behind the solidified clamp of my throat.

He pressed his face harder against mine, tears running between our compressed skin.

I felt him lift into the space above me, the sound of shouting echoing through my skull like an explosion.

In the distance, I could see the remaining bodies scooping up garments and disappearing into the shadows. The sound of panic and shock accented the audible scurrying.

"Fuck!" I heard Paul scream, a loud crash following his outburst.

In the ever-clearing, sloth-like crawl of the haze, I could see Gauge pounding his fists into Paul. Paul's head jolted from side to side with each of the forceful blows.

I could feel my head beginning to respond to my brain's command to move, when I was scooped from the wooden spool and carried to the couch. I could feel my underwear and jeans being lifted over my legs and pulled to my hips. I saw Paul, a bloodied stump in the corner of the room, as Gauge lifted my shoulders to put on my shirt.

I stared in a dreamlike silence as I watched Gauge disappear into the bedroom, reappearing a few minutes later with our oversized knapsack.

He pulled me from the couch and into his arms, the striking outline of a pendulum etched over the surface of the spool filling my vision as we moved through the room.

I could hear Gauge's feet scuffing the narrow stairs as we descended to the first level of the building. Kicking open the front door, the vacuum-like suction of the desert air pulled at us as we walked down the sidewalk.

He sat me beside him as he fidgeted with the lock and chain, freeing the Indian and moving it from the sidewalk to the street.

My eyes continued to waver in clarity as I saw him fasten the knapsack to the back of the bike. Placing one of the helmets over my head, he pulled me against his chest, stood to his full height, and carefully boarded the Indian. Tucked between his arms, he secured my limp body against him before kick-starting the engine. I felt the motorcycle vibrate into the dry night air as the world around me went black and I once again fell into the unwelcome arms of unconsciousness.

***

I AWOKE TO THE sound of Gauge frantically shuffling through the knapsack.

"Babe," he said, noticing that I was awake. I found myself seated beside the Indian, where it was parked before an old-fashioned gas pump.

I trailed my eyes over the scene before me, the purple glow of the rising sun painting over the desert horizon like a silk curtain.

"The money, babe. Where's the money?"

The panic in Gauge's voice sobered my lingering haze. I took a deep breath and stood to my feet, a slight dizziness spinning around my head like a dozen or so flies surrounding a freshly smashed roadside carcass.

"Here," I croaked, my voice dry and painfully hollow, "let me find it."

Gauge stepped aside as I swept through the giant knapsack with both hands. Complacency became horror as I realized that none of the divvied-out, hidden stashes of cash remained where I had stored them. Our money was gone. All of it. Gone.

"Fuck!" Gauge shouted when I looked at him, my face confirming his fear. "Those motherfuckers! We have to go back. We have to get our money."

"No!" I screamed, the sudden power of my voice both surprising and excruciating. "We can't go back there."

He stared at me for a long moment before tossing his hands into the air.

"Then how the fuck are we gonna keep going, Dustin?" he cried, panic frozen across his expression. "We need gas, and we have no money. Nothing!"

I lowered my eyes to the ground. Witnessing Gauge's extreme reaction had signaled a void of defeat within me. I felt my brain firing off clouded ideas that I couldn't comprehend. The lingering effect of whatever I had been drugged with still clouded the blood in my veins like spilled oil over the surface of the sea. As much as I tried, I couldn't think. Just standing and slightly speaking had worked my current cognitive ability to its capacity.

"I need water," I whispered, my voice too dry and cracked for use.

Gauge looked up at me, his eyes wide, as though he only just now realized I was awake.

"Babe," he said softly, pulling me into his arms. "I'm so sorry. I'm just scared. I don't know what to do."

I opened my eyes, spying what appeared to be a water pump standing beside a rundown outhouse.

"Water," I choked, pulling from Gauge's embrace and shuffling toward the pump.

"Let me help you," Gauge offered, grabbing my hand in his.

A churning flow of desperation zipped through my core as I watched Gauge lift and lower the pump handle with all his strength. Nothing happened.

A tear jumped from my eye as I turned to look away. Never in my life had I experienced such a longing thirst. It felt as though my insides had become as dry and barren as the endless, dehydrated ground that spread for miles beneath our feet.

"Y'all all right?" a soft voice asked.

I looked up to see the gas station attendant, her brown hair wrapped in a bun, her gentle face glowing yet makeup free.

"Can I help you boys with something?"

Gauge dropped the pump handle, its fruitless labor heaving one final squeal into the dawning of the day.

"I need water," I whispered, the walls of my throat aching as though the glide of my breath were somehow scraping and tearing at its dried lining.

I watched as her face shuffled from a look of puzzlement to one of fear and concern.

"I think you boys need to go," she said, her attention locked on Gauge.

I followed her stare, realizing her eyes were fixed upon the splattered blood that spread over Gauge's white undershirt. I too was shocked by the crimson stains that streaked across the fabric as if left by the hoofprints of some dancing demon.

"Are we able to get him some water?" Gauge asked, nodding toward me.

The attendant followed his movement, locking her eyes onto mine, her brain scanning my face for any visible signs of danger.

"What's going on?" she asked, bringing her attention back to Gauge. "Why are you bleeding?"

Gauge looked down at his shirt, pulling it forward so that he could view it better. It was obvious that he was just as surprised at the presence of the blood as the attendant.

"We were robbed," I managed to choke out, my voice rough and waterless.

"Oh dear," the tiny woman replied, her eyes widening in horror.

"Please," she began, motioning for us to follow her. "I have water in my cooler. Let's get you two cleaned up and situated."

We followed her to the back of the tiny building that housed the cashier counter. Pulling open a small door, she leaned down to a small white cooler, retrieving several thermoses of different sizes and color.

"Here," she said softly, placing the largest of the plastic containers into my hand. "Please, drink all of it. It's okay."

She handed one to Gauge, eyeing him slowly as he took it from her grasp.

"Where you boys headed?"

"LA," answered Gauge, removing his shirt and dropping it to the ground. "You have some place I can toss that?"

The attendant stared at him, her eyes bouncing between his as if viewing a tennis match on fast-forward.

"I don't know if that's a good idea," she replied, allowing her eyes to drift down Gauge's exposed torso and to the crumpled T-shirt on the ground.

"Why?" Gauge asked, tilting his head to the side.

"I am not comfortable with having something with blood all over it on the premises," she responded, keeping her eyes fixed on the fallen garment. "Not that I don't believe you or anything, I would just rather not have it here."

"Fair enough," Gauge replied, sighing. "I'll keep it with me."

"We have no money," I chimed in, absorbing the final drops of the thermos. "They took everything."

The attendant stared at me, her bouncing gaze now attempting to read my thoughts.

"I see," she finally responded after a long hesitation.

"We need gas, though," Gauge added. "We could work for it."

The woman stepped back so she could eye both Gauge and me at the same time. It was obvious that she was listening to several thoughts at once, seemingly searching for the certain tone of her inner voice.

"No," she declared. "You can't work for it."

Gauge sighed and leaned down to retrieve his shirt. I started to follow him as he began to shuffle back toward the front of the gas station.

"I will just fill it for you."

We stopped, stunned by her unexpected offer.

"I can tell you boys have been through something," she continued, her voice wavering slightly. "I know what it's like to be robbed. It's happened to me here on more than one occasion. It's terrifying and invasive. I would never wish it on anyone. So I feel like the good Lord wants me to help you."

We could only stare at her, both of us at a loss for words.

"Just go back to the pump, and I'll turn it on."

I lost my breath, my emotion making way for tears of relief.

"God bless you both," she concluded, smiling as she handed me the remaining thermos in her hand.

"Thank you," I whispered, my voice carried off by the strengthening desert wind.

She nodded, turned to close the small door, and then made her way to the side of the building.

Gauge topped off the tank as I chugged the second thermos. Though I was steadily drinking, I couldn't quench my seemingly endless thirst.

Hopping behind Gauge as he steadied the bike, he started the rejuvenated engine and throttled us out onto the open road.

I rested my head against his back, listening to the gentle beating of his heart as it rivaled the deafening groan of the motorcycle's engine. I closed my eyes as the sun continued to rise above us, the promise of its relentless glare fulfilled by the absence of a single cloud. I exhaled, uncaring as to how much further we had to go. Instead, I just rode.

***

WE BROKE DOWN JUST outside of Barstow, California. I watched in an exhausted silence as Gauge cursed, kicked, and fiddled with the smoking Indian. It had begun to stutter not long after we left the gas station, evolving into a consistent, stammered choking that resulted in the engine overheating and us being stranded on the roadside.

I stood still as several big rig trucks sailed past us. I was tempted to flag one down.

"What are we going to do?" I asked, squatting beside Gauge.

"What do you think we are gonna do?" he responded, his frustration and annoyance clear. "We're gonna have to walk."

"We could try and get someone to stop," I suggested, turning my head back toward the road.

"Let's not count on that," Gauge replied, standing to his feet. "Let's just face it and go. We don't have that much further before we get to this next town."

I dreaded the walk. My head continued to spin, and my thirst remained unquenched. I didn't say anything to Gauge, but I felt that whatever drug I had been given was still very potent within my bloodstream. Several times during the ride, my dizziness had become so overwhelming that I nearly fell off the bike. I didn't want to worry Gauge. Plus, there was nothing either of us could do about it anyway.

We entered Barstow after an hour's walk in the scorching desert heat. Gauge pushed the Indian while I taxied the knapsack. I swore it was filled with iron weights by the time we entered town. Stopping at a small gas station, I quietly tiptoed behind the building to vomit while Gauge searched for the attendant.

I didn't tell him what had happened. Apparently, the station was closed, and we were forced to keep walking.

Motels and fast food restaurants lined the main street of Barstow. Facing heat stroke and exhaustion, we stopped at one of the motels. Gauge went inside the office while I snuck behind a tree to vomit again. Without food or water, I began to produce nothing but a brown bile. I thought I saw a trace of blood, but I wasn't certain.

Gauge reappeared, a worried look accenting his tired face.

"The office called the police," he announced, exhaling loudly as he sat beside the Indian.

"What for?" I asked, quietly wiping some lingering saliva from my chin.

"I told him we were broke down and broke, and he said the police would be the best option for help."

"Well, don't you think they might ask a lot of questions? I mean, what if Paul called the police in Vegas? What if we're wanted?"

Gauge lifted his eyes to mine, his weary gaze heavy and weighted.

"Calm down," he answered. "Do you really think Paul is going to call the cops after he drugged you and tried doing whatever the fuck it was they were doing in their little devil orgy?"

I nodded, realizing he was right. My brain was too heated and my stomach too upset for proper thought. I moved to join him beside the bike.

"What's that smell?" Gauge asked, moving his head toward mine.

"What smell?" I replied coyly.

"Something smells like puke. Did you throw up?"

He drifted his nose a few centimeters from my lips, confirming his suspicion.

"You did," he answered himself. "Are you okay?"

"Yes, yes," I responded, embarrassed that he caught me. "I think it's just the heat."

He stared at me, his eyes reading mine.

"You're not okay," he replied, lifting his hand to my forehead. "Dustin, you are burning up!"

"Well, of course I am, Gauge. How else do you think I am going to feel after walking miles in over a hundred-degree heat?"

He moved his hand around my face, pressing his lips to my forehead when his fingers no longer provided enough information.

"No, Dustin," he said softly. "You have a fever."

I looked at him, too exhausted to argue and too scared to deny the truth.

Before anything more could be said, a sole police cruiser pulled in front of us.

"Is there something I can help you boys with?" a gruff voice asked.

I didn't move as Gauge stood to greet him.

"We broke down, officer," he started, leaning against the open passenger side window. "We've been walking for miles. Someone slipped our cash out of our pack somewhere along the way. We're kinda stranded."

I couldn't see the officer from the ground, but I could hear him begin to fidget with his police radio. He murmured some abbreviated jargon before responding to Gauge.

"Is that your bike?" I heard him ask.

"Yes, sir," Gauge replied, turning his head toward the Indian.

" '49 Indian?" the officer asked.

"Yeah," Gauge answered, his voice lifting with a bit of inter-est. "You know motorcycles?"

"My dad had a '49 Indian. Just like that one. His was blue. I've been trying to get my hands on one for years."

The radio began to crackle and mumble.

"This one was my pop's," Gauge replied. "I've been slowly restoring it. Takes a lot more work than you think."

"Oh, tell me about it, son," the officer laughed, his gruff voice both comforting and slightly alarming. "It's an old piece now, you pretty much have to replace everything."

The chit-chat regarding the Indian continued for about ten minutes. Finally, the officer called a tow truck and asked us into his cruiser.

"Is there someone you'd like to call?" the officer asked as we climbed into the backseat.

"Uh, no," Gauge responded, looking out the back window at the tow truck driver, who was slowly finishing up with the Indian.

"Here's the deal," the officer started. "I'm going to take you boys down to the station. I have to do a report on this. You're not in trouble or anything. It's just a formality."

I looked over at Gauge, who kept his eyes focused on the officer's, which peered back at him through the rearview mirror.

"But then you boys are going to have to come up with a plan," he continued, shifting his eyes over to mine. "Where are you going to stay tonight?"

Gauge and I looked at each other, both too tired and caught up in the day's events to fathom any form of proper response.

"Okay, look," the officer continued. "Byron, the tow truck driver, will take a look at the Indian for free. He will do it for me. I can't have you boys stranded on the streets, though. I can let you both crash in the loft of my garage, but you need to make some calls or figure out some way to be on your way."

"Thank you, officer," Gauge said, clearing his throat from both nerves and heat. "We'll figure something out. I promise."

"Jenkins," the officer replied. "Tyrone Jenkins."

"Thank you, Officer Jenkins," Gauge retorted, smiling as the officer nodded his approval in the mirror.

***

AFTER AN HOUR AT the station, Officer Jenkins stopped off at a small diner, its décor and vibe heavy on the nostalgia. Each staff member greeted the officer as we entered, bee-lining for what I imagined was the officer's designated booth.

"I come here all the time," he announced as we sat. "Best pancakes this side of the country. I swear it."

I glanced at the menu, the description of each of the entrees twisting and squeezing my churning stomach into tighter knots.

"You boys just get whatever you want," Officer Jenkins continued. "I can tell you have had a day of it."

"Well, look who it is," a high-pitched voice chimed. "Geez, Tyrone, it's been what, eight hours since I saw you last?"

The waitress was a short woman, boisterous and heavy set. Her face was caked with makeup, as though a child had brushed every color in its paint palette across her skin. Her appearance was both charming and disturbing.

"Yeah, yeah," Officer Jenkins laughed. "These are some boys I found stranded out on Main. Poor guys have been pushing a heavy-ass motorcycle for miles."

"Heavens!" the woman cried in what appeared to be genuine shock. "Well, say no more. Let me get you boys some water."

She disappeared behind a distant pastry counter.

"That's Pamela," Officer Jenkins revealed in a low voice. "She's had the hots for me for about twenty years now. Poor thing. One of these days, I'll just have to throw her a bone and ask her out."

Gauge and I only stared.

"Hell, with that kabuki face, I'd be afraid to go any place where they might mistake her for an escaped clown."

He laughed at his own joke, clearing his throat in an attempt to regain his composure as he realized neither Gauge nor I responded.

"Anyway," he continued, smoothing out his menu with his hands. "She's a good girl. Kooky as all get out, but with a good heart."

"Here we go!" Pamela announced as she rounded the corner with a tray full of condensation-heavy glasses of ice water. "Please, drink up!"

She watched with a careful smile as Gauge and I downed two glasses each. I felt my stomach jump and waver at the sudden invasion of the ice-cold liquid. I closed my eyes in an attempt to mentally stabilize the feeling.

"Well now, what will you hungry fellas be having?"

As Officer Jenkins and Gauge rattled off their orders, the visual image of each selection mentioned flashed before my eyes, its appearance and smell so vivid in my mind that I could nearly touch and taste it. By the time Pamela made it to me, I was covered in vomit.

"Oh dear!" she exclaimed, stepping back to avoid what had spilled to the floor.

I felt Gauge grab me, wiping my face with a napkin.

Officer Jenkins stood up as Pamela ran to fetch some rags. They both stared in silence as Gauge carefully cleaned me, cycling the rags over my face and shirt until each was weighted with the contents of the mess.

Their words became muffled as I was shuffled back to the police cruiser. I wasn't able to hear clearly again until we reached a nearby clinic.

"What is your name?" a short, mustached man asked me, his face so close to mine that I could smell chocolate on his breath.

"Gauge," I replied, my voice strained and sore.

There was a commotion before the doctor's face reappeared.

"That is not your name. What is your name?"

I closed my eyes as my head began to spin. Thoughts and images passed before the screen behind my lids like a film projector gone mad. It wasn't until Gauge gripped my face in his hands that the spinning stopped.

"Dustin," I heard him say. "You have to focus now. Look at me, Dustin. Focus."

His face began to clear the longer I stared. The intense look of concern and fear that stretched over his expression sent an alarmed jolt through my heart. I had never seen him so terrified.

"Okay," I whispered.

The world continued in a shadowed haze as the doctor diagnosed me with severe heat exhaustion and recited a list of home instructions.

I felt Gauge carefully guiding me as we exited the cruiser at Officer Jenkin's house. I could hear him and the officer chatting briefly as I was led to a small bed in the corner of a garage. The smell of old oil and burnt rubber filled the air like an unmoving cloud. I closed my eyes and fell into a very deep sleep, not waking or moving for what must have been hours.

***

IT WAS PITCH BLACK when I opened my eyes. I looked around, searching for a trace of light, but found only darkness. I began to panic as I slid my hands beside me, drifting them into the unseen distance. My right hand felt a wall, my left found Gauge's thigh.

"What's wrong?" he whispered, jumping into a sitting position. I could tell that I had woken him.

"Are you okay, baby?" he asked, lowering his face to mine. "Do you need anything? What's the matter?"

The panicked race of my heart slowed as the warm, familiar smell of his breath caressed my face. I was focused on controlling my breathing, when I felt him lift me from the pillow.

"Here, babe," he said, placing a cold drinking glass to my lips. "You need water."

Carefully, he tipped my head back with the glass, ensuring a mouthful before lowering both to center.

"How're you feeling?" he asked, the sound of his voice wrapping around me like a warm and welcome blanket.

"Better," I whispered, my stomach churning from the water. "Where's the bathroom?"

Gauge fumbled in the darkness, eventually producing a small flashlight. A dim yellow beam led the way as he guided me slowly toward a small door in the corner of the loft.

I closed the door behind me, barely making it in time as I sat on the toilet. A singular bulb provided a soft light as the contents of my bowels groaned and splashed into the commode. The smell was rancid, my eyes watering from both the putrid stench and the ache of my convulsing torso.

"Babe," Gauge said in horror, dropping to his knees beside me. I didn't realize he had opened the small bathroom door. "We need to get you to a hospital."

I shook my head, grimacing as more fluid escaped into the bowl.

"No," I managed to whisper. "No more hospitals."

"But, babe, you're really sick, we need to–"

"It's just exhaustion," I interrupted, my voice finding volume and control. "Heat exhaustion, you heard the doctor."

I didn't listen as Gauge continued to suggest further medical intervention. Instead, I closed my eyes as he leaned me forward to clean my backside. Never in my life had I felt so completely helpless.

Leading me back to the bed, he tucked me in and sat beside me. I drifted to sleep knowing he wouldn't find slumber for himself. Instead, he would remain awake the rest of the night, lovingly and carefully observing me until the dawn.

***

ONE WEEK LATER AND I was feeling a bit better. I still suffered near-constant nausea and an unrelenting dizziness, but at least I was now able to hold down solid food. My bowel movements remained inconsistent and watery, but I could manage as long as I was no longer vomiting everything that went into my stomach.

Thanks to Officer Jenkins, I was washing dishes at the small diner, while Gauge was assisting Byron at his auto shop. This way, we could save a bit of money to help get us back on the road to LA.

This time around, the Indian only needed a few minor repairs, and Byron had agreed to let Gauge work off the parts and labor it would require.

When we weren't working, we were together in Officer Jenkins's lawn, gazing at the brilliant display of stars above us. It was amazing how intense and beautiful the night sky was in the desert. Much like the stars above the Everglades back home, each flickering dazzle of light appeared to shimmer its glow as if vying for individual attention. Gauge would tease and taunt my fear of stories about spacecraft and aliens. He would joke that they would more than likely visit us in the night, carrying us off to some secret location far within the desert, performing painful and invasive experiments on us the way schoolchildren dissect dead frogs in a science lab.

Officer Jenkins remained helpful and friendly. He gave us rides to our jobs each morning, always dropping Gauge off first so he could stay at the diner to eat his breakfast after we arrived.

I was becoming close with Pamela, her joyful laughter and cheery disposition hypnotic and inviting. A perk of my job was access to leftover food items, but I often found myself wrapping them up to take home to Gauge, as my appetite had dwindled to near depletion.

The heat exhaustion had completely annihilated my system. From the top of my head down to the tips of my toes, I felt an off-key presence. It was as if the spiked drink had made way for some sort of infection or illness to enter my body, or perhaps weakened my system enough to expose one that was already present. Whatever the case, I had not felt like myself since before we left Las Vegas.

It was a Friday night when I decided not to wait for Officer Jenkins and ventured the short trek home alone. Gauge was already there when I arrived. The Indian, freshly washed and polished, gleamed in the faint light of the setting sun.

"She's up and running, babe!" he announced excitedly as I walked up the driveway. "She will have us purring into LA like movie stars!"

I smiled, entertained and comforted at Gauge's unfaltering enthusiasm. At this point, not making it to LA would seem like the definite end of the universe.

"She looks amazing, babe," I replied, holding up a plastic bag full of Styrofoam food containers. "Dinner."

"Mmm," he said, his eyes watered with hunger. "Thanks, babe."

I walked inside the garage and made my way to the loft. As I was rounding the thin wall that separated the two areas, I felt my vision begin to sway and my stomach churn and gurgle. I managed to flip the light switch on just as I relieved myself from both ends. Instantly, the room smelled of a putrid mixture of excrement and bile. The involuntary action brought me to my knees in tears.

I couldn't move as I knelt within the puddle of my own filth. It was several minutes before Gauge came to look for me.

"Babe!" he shouted, falling against my back. "Oh my God, babe! What happened? What's going on?"

I stared in a stunned silence as tears quickly edged his lower lids. They began to fall as he lifted me from my pool of shame and onto the bed.

I could only watch as he hastily mopped the floor and stripped off my clothing. He carried me to the small bathroom, which touted a tiny walk-in shower, and placed me within it. I didn't flinch as a blast of cold water iced over me without warning. Gauge scrubbed my body as the water slowly began to warm.

We didn't speak as he dried and carried me back to the bed. Dressing me quickly, he lifted me into his arms and began walking toward the Indian. Officer Jenkins was pulling in just as we exited the garage.

"What's the matter?" he asked, popping out of his cruiser like a curious mongoose from its burrow.

"I need to get him to the hospital," Gauge announced, adjusting my weight in his arms. "Not the clinic. The hospital. He's burning up with fever."

"Here," Officer Jenkins replied, opening the back door of his police car. "Lay him in here."

The ride to the hospital was nauseating and terrifying. What was wrong with me? How could a drug linger in my system for so long? Was it something else? Did I have some aggressive stomach flu that wouldn't let up? I didn't know, yet in my worried confusion, I could only think of my mother.

The small community hospital was quaint and efficient. Either due to the severity of my condition or the presence of Officer Jenkins, we sailed past the congregation of the waiting area and directly into an examining room.

A nurse took my vital signs as Gauge and Officer Jenkins briefed her on my symptoms. I drifted in and out of consciousness as we waited for a doctor.

When I came to, I was in a hospital bed, a plastic bracelet secured around my wrist, a starched, stiff blue gown draped over the front of my body. I looked around the small room, the contents sparse and sterile. I saw Gauge piled into a chair beside me, his knees tucked against his chest, his head resting on his shoulder. He looked to be asleep.

"Babe," I whispered, my voice too weak and broken to speak.

Instantly, he lifted his head and looked at me, a slight drapery of sleep clouding his eyes.

"Hey," he said, lowering his feet to the floor and inching toward me. "How are you feeling?"

"What's wrong? What have they found out?" I asked, my heart beginning to race with the pace of each speeding thought. I was terrified to hear what Gauge was about to tell me.

"Whoa, whoa," he cooed. "Calm down, baby. It's just a stomach bug."

An immeasurable ton lifted from my chest. Relief poured over me and through my veins like a welcome rain.

"They are running more tests, but the doctor is sure you've just been dealing with a really nasty stomach flu."

I sighed as he placed a hand over my cheek. I closed my eyes and pressed my face into his touch, allowing the familiar warmth of his skin to ease my rambling mind.

"They hooked you to an IV," Gauge spoke gently, allowing his voice to accent the soothing touch of his hand. "You were severely dehydrated. The doctor said it could also be your body adjusting to the heat here."

He smiled as I opened my eyes. I gazed at him lovingly as he continued to speak.

"It was hot back home in Florida, but not like this, right? It's like someone left a giant oven on around here or something. I've never felt anything so damn hot and dry. It's like being cooked alive. I'm like, 'Give me some humidity!' Right?"

I closed my eyes and smiled as I rested my face back against his still open hand. The smell of his sweat and skin seeped into my brain like a lifesaving medicine.

We sat and chatted for what seemed like hours. Finally, a tall woman entered the room, her face defined by a pair of enormous eyeglasses, her auburn hair piled high above her head, and her magnified gaze highlighted by the batting heaviness of her chunky mascara. She looked like an exaggerated cartoon character.

"Mr. Thomas," she spoke sternly, reaching her hand for mine as she moved toward me. "I am Dr. Hembold."

Her grip was firm and solid. She pursed her lips as our eyes met. She shot a suspicious glance at Gauge before taking a step backward.

"We are still running some tests, but it appears that you are suffering some sort of stomach virus."

She adjusted her giant-framed glasses as she peered over a chart in her hand.

"Once the bloodwork comes back, we will have you up and on your way."

She closed the folder and paused, keeping her eyes down. After a long moment, she took a deep breath and lifted her face.

"I haven't formally asked your relation to Mr. Thomas," she stated, her bug-like eyes fixed on Gauge. "I know we have spoken already, but I am just curious as to who you are."

Gauge stared back at her, raising his head in what appeared to be defiant pride.

"I," he stated, turning his head toward me, "am the love of his life."

I laughed and smiled, placing a hand over my face in embarrassment. When I brought my attention back to the room, I saw a reactionless Dr. Hembold glaring at us both. I reached over and punched Gauge's arm, halting his ongoing laughter.

"I see," she remarked coldly, dropping the folder to her side. "I will have the nurse return in a moment. I am going to need a bit more bloodwork for some final tests."

"I thought you said you were already waiting on bloodwork?" Gauge questioned. "Why do you need more?"

Dr. Hembold continued to stare at him, her magnified eyes beaming with disapproval and judgment.

"I have decided to order a new test. There are some other variables that may be affecting Dustin's health, and I would like to see if they are contributing factors."

Gauge looked at me as I continued to stare at the doctor. Her words were coated in suspicion and accusation. The lingering presence of some form of unspoken omen began to pollute the air of the room like the stench outside of a chemical plant.

"I will be back in a few hours to check in."

The doctor continued to stare, her giant eyes moving between us like one of those art deco kit-cat clocks.

"What's with her?" Gauge asked as he took his seat after the doctor had exited the room. "Since when does a stomach flu require so much blood testing?"

I didn't answer. Something inside me, that quiet, still inner voice, began sending veiled messages of panic and alarm. I couldn't understand or even begin to process them clearly, so I simply let them be.

Once more, I was a victim to my lack of health insurance. The doctor returned one last time, assured that my symptoms had subsided, and then filed for my discharge.

I was quiet during the car ride home. Officer Jenkins and Gauge chatted aimlessly in the front seat of the cruiser as I allowed my mind to wander out over the endless miles of surrounding desert.

Like the dry and rambling tumbleweed, a constant and gnawing feeling rolled around inside my core, pricking and scraping everything it touched. As we turned the final corner toward Officer Jenkins's house, I knew with certainty that I would hear from Dr. Hembold again. It would be then that the dark and sinister feeling within would be revealed.

***

THE NEXT FEW WEEKS were wonderful. Slowly saving money, Gauge and I finally felt free to venture out and enjoy small, inexpensive escapades. Spending only a few dollars in gas, we would cruise the Indian out into the desert, following some desolate, worn roadway for miles on end.

On one particular journey, Gauge brought along the knapsack, its bursting contents a mystery to me. No matter what, Gauge would not let me peek inside the heavy, worn pack. Instead, it rested securely behind me on the bike as we rumbled down another endless stretch of cracked desert highway.

The sun was setting when we finally pulled over to rest.

"So," Gauge started, unstrapping the knapsack from the Indian, "ready to see what's inside?"

I smiled and nodded.

Grinning like a kid on Christmas morning, Gauge unbuckled the single strap of the bag and emptied the confidential materials onto the ground. A green tarp and a large bundle of blankets flopped open over the dirt. I looked up at Gauge, who was already beaming at me, his eyes glinting in the orange glow of the fading sunlight.

"We're gonna camp here, babe," he announced when I failed to respond. "I brought everything. I found this old army tent in Tyrone's garage, and I have enough blankets to keep us both warm. I even brought some food to roast over the fire."

I smiled at him, the look of pure excitement plastered across his face contagious, if not slightly pathetic. I wasn't thrilled with the notion of sleeping on the hard desert ground when we had a perfectly comfortable bed back at Officer Jenkins's but I could easily see how much this plan and gesture meant to Gauge.

"Aw, babe. Thank you," I finally responded, moving to kiss him.

I was delegated to stick-gathering duty while Gauge situated the tent. Pitched between a family of cacti, it was a picturesque and ideal camping setup.

Smiling to myself, I stacked the sticks into a neat pile and carefully unwrapped the foil-covered hotdogs and cheese Gauge had brought along to cook.

With the sun now set, Gauge ignited the fire, and we cozied up together to watch it burn.

The smell of the hotdogs roasting over the open flame made my stomach queasy. I was still not feeling 100 percent, but I was managing to keep down most everything I ate and drank. It seemed the persistent stomach flu had finally been overtaken by my immune system.

"Here we are, baby," Gauge boasted cheerfully as he handed me a charred hotdog with melted cheese blanketed over it. "Sorry, I couldn't locate any bread. But who cares, right? The meat and cheese is always the best part anyway."

I chuckled and pulled the hotdog from the stick. I felt my stomach grip and grumble as soon I swallowed the first bite. My nerves began to peak as I realized I was completely without any form of proper restroom facility if I were to become sick. The idea of puking or shitting next to a cactus was not appealing, to say the least.

Thankfully, my digestive system seemed to calm itself, and I was able to enjoy the rest of the evening in peace.

Together beneath the celestial sky, Gauge and I embraced under a blanket, watching the glittering dance of the heavens as it ebbed and flowed over the desert.

"It's so awesome," Gauge whispered, pulling me closer to him. The warmth of his body seemed to lull and ease my wariness concerning my stomach. "I couldn't imagine being here with anyone but you, babe."

I smiled and nuzzled my nose against his neck.

"I haven't had the chance to say thank you," he continued, his voice becoming stern and serious. "The way you cared for me when I got hurt. The way you took care of everything and made sure we got here safe."

I could hear his breathing succumb to a change in emotion.

"I've never had anyone care for me the way you do. I can honestly say that no one has ever loved me the way you do."

I stayed quiet as he spoke, feeling the change in his heartbeat as it increased from a soft patter to a racing pace.

"And I know that I have never loved anyone the way I love you," he continued, a tear falling from his cheek and onto mine. "You're my world, Dustin."

The mingling tears followed gravity's pull to the dry earth below us.

"I love you too, Gauge. I have from the moment I first laid eyes on you."

He squeezed me tighter, the beating of our hearts seeming to pound in unison.

We didn't speak for the rest of the night. Instead, we simply held each other, listening to the night song of the desert as it harmonized around us. Eventually, we moved into the small covering of the tent and fell asleep.

I opened my eyes just as the sun began to peek above the distant mountain tops. I looked over at Gauge, his soft, youthful face glowing in the faint light. As I watched him gently breathe, I listened to the confirmation of my heart as it validated what I had known from the very first time I ever saw him: this man, the one sleeping softly beside me, was the love of my life.

***

A WEEK LATER, WE had saved enough to leave. Gauge and I spent two hours preparing a roast beef dinner for Officer Jenkins. It was our only way to thank him for his hospitality, and with the quality of Gauge's cooking skills, it was a far better gesture than any gift or card could provide.

I was chopping the vegetables while Gauge focused on the roast, when Officer Jenkins arrived.

"Well, damn," he declared as he entered the small kitchen. "I have not smelled a homecooked meal as fine as this since I left my momma's house thirty years ago."

Gauge and I smiled, carefully tending to our work.

With the meal prepared, the three of us sat around Officer Jenkins's oak kitchen table. Gauge and the officer downed several beers with their dinner, while I sipped a glass of water. I didn't tell Gauge, but my diarrhea was back. Yesterday morning, I had a bowl of cereal at the diner, which ended up in the toilet just minutes later. I wasn't certain, but I swore I saw blood in the bowl before I flushed.

"Oh, before I forget," Officer Jenkins said between he and Gauge's laughter, "Dr. Hembold needs to see you tomorrow, Dustin. She has some more of your bloodwork back. She said it was important."

I stared at him, his words dripping over me like hot candle wax. My stomach began to churn and bubble as my inner voice again whispered its faint warnings of dread.

"Okay," I smiled, spying Gauge's concerned look in the corner of my eye.

"I'll give you a lift, first thing," Officer Jenkins offered. "Did you tell Pamela you were leaving?"

The rest of the evening consisted of endless talk of the Indian. Officer Jenkins was in love with the bike. On more than one occasion, Gauge let the man speed off with it into the sunset after he returned home from a shift. Just as with Gauge and his dad, Officer Jenkins appeared to silently connect his own father to the motorcycle. There was a look of serenity on his face whenever he rode it, almost as though he were somehow transported back in time to his childhood, long before he became a police officer and experienced firsthand the depravity and darkness of the human condition.

When we finally went to bed, Officer Jenkins hugged us both, thanked us for the dinner, and watched as we made our way to the garage.

Gauge made love to me that night, but the physical movement was dizzying and painful. I didn't say a word as I cleaned myself in the bathroom afterward, the presence of blood splattered across the toilet paper as expected as it was frightening.

***

"DO YOU WANT ME to come in with you?" Officer Jenkins asked as we pulled in front of the community hospital the next morning.

"No," I answered, gazing at the small white building through the fog of the car window.

"So Gauge is picking you up?" the officer confirmed, his voice reverting to police mode from casual friendship.

"Yeah," I replied, "I told him to be here in an hour."

Gauge wanted to come, but I didn't let him. I knew that whatever Dr. Hembold was about to tell me, I would need to hear it alone before involving Gauge.

"All right, my friend," Officer Jenkins said, reaching out his hand. "I am sure gonna miss you boys. You really added a bit of life to my ol' boring-ass world."

I shook his hand and smiled, glimpsing my nervous expression in the reflection of his dark brown eyes.

"You boys call me if you need anything before you head out. And please remember to hit me up from time to time."

I nodded, pulling the door handle with my free hand.

"And, Dustin"—his voice stopped my movement. I turned back to face him—"don't get too famous out there in ol' Hollyweird."

I laughed politely, my pathetic response camouflaged by his own boisterous laughter.

I waved as I walked the short distance between the driveway and the front entrance. Officer Jenkins waved back, ensured that I made it inside safely, and then pulled the police cruiser into the dawning of the day.

My heart froze when I realized Dr. Hembold was waiting for me at the entrance.

"Hello, Dustin," she greeted me dryly as the automatic doors slid shut behind me. "Please, follow me to my office."

My heart deafened my hearing as I followed the tall woman down a small hallway and through an open door.

"Please, have a seat," she directed, waving her arm to a set of chairs in front of a small, sparsely decorated desk.

"Have you ever heard of the gay cancer, Mr. Thomas?"

My heart seemed to stop beating as her words absorbed into my brain. I followed her lead and sat in one of the chairs.

"AIDS, Mr. Thomas?" she continued when I didn't give her an answer.

"Um, I think so," I replied meekly, my only knowledge of the term from that of droning dinner table conversations between my parents, and a jumbled collection of brief news reports I had viewed on television.

"Don't worry," Dr. Hembold continued, flipping through the pages in the folder on her lap. "I do not know if you have it or not. There is a new blood test for it, but our lab doesn't have access to it yet."

I stared at her blankly, completely unsure as to the meaning of what she was saying.

"I was able to run some other standard tests, though. Something is compromising your immune system. Your T-cells are low."

She stared at me as I attempted to make sense of what she was trying to tell me.

"What I am suggesting, Mr. Thomas, is that you and your boyfriend get tested for HIV, the virus that causes AIDS."

Silence.

"It is a gay-related disease. It is highly possible that you are both infected."

My heart reignited its racing pulse as her words began to make sense. I didn't know enough about the virus to be certain, but from what I did know, I knew there wasn't an easy solution.

"I don't understand," I finally mumbled, forcing my voice over the relentless pound of my heart. "I thought it was something drug-related, like with needles and stuff."

"That is true," she confirmed, her stone-cold eyes slowly scanning my face. "But it seems to have originated with gay men. We now know that it is sexually transmitted."

We stared at each other, neither speaking nor blinking.

"I will be frank, Mr. Thomas," she sighed, slowly pushing her oversized glasses up her slender nose. "We all face the consequences of our actions in life."

She waited for me to respond, but I could only continue to stare, my voice locked beneath the weight of the avalanche of my thoughts and emotions.

"Perhaps this disease is nature's way of correcting an immoral and unnatural injustice. Simply put, Dustin, maybe this is Mother Nature's way of ridding that which offends her."

Flashed images of my mother's cruel and angered expression shot before my eyes like a rifle's laser. It was almost as though my mother herself were somewhere in the room, watching, disapproving.

"From a medical perspective, homosexual intercourse is anything but natural."

She closed the folder and adjusted her height in the chair.

"It would seem that this disease is the consequence of those unnatural actions and choices. You have a choice, Mr. Thomas. We all do."

Tears began to cloud my eyes as I listened to her words become heavier and more accusatory. It was when she began lecturing me about the perils of promiscuous sex that I stopped her.

"You know nothing about me," I said, seething with a sudden anger. "I am not promiscuous. Neither is Gauge. We have both only been with each other."

She stared at me coldly, her enlarged eyes sterile and vacant.

"So, you can think whatever you want, but my life has been nothing like what you just described."

I stood from my chair, anger leading me to the door.

"I would think that as a medical professional, you would be a bit more open-minded and compassionate."

I turned the knob and began to open the door.

"Not everyone lives inside a one-size-fits-all box."

I started to exit when she stopped me.

"You are so naive," she said softly, shaking her head. "You have no idea what this disease brings. You are just a little boy."

I turned to face her, instinctively closing the door behind me.

"We can't stop this. There is no cure."

Her eyes seemed to dazzle as she spoke, almost as though tears were beginning to gather.

"People are dying by the thousands, and there is nothing the medical world can do but watch."

She stood and moved to her desk.

"As a medical professional, it is horrifying."

She sat in the desk chair, her posture firm and tall.

"But as a woman of faith..."

She paused, allowing her words to float around me until I had processed and echoed each syllable within my head.

"Well, from that perspective, I just see it as you people getting what's coming to you."

She locked eyes with mine, her cartoonish stare now appearing dark and sinister.

"Frankly, my dear," she began, pursing her lips when she paused, "you will get what you deserve."

A tear fell from my eye as I turned to leave the room. I could hear Dr. Hembold shouting at me as I made my way down the small hallway and out the large automatic glass doors. Gauge was waiting in the driveway.

"What's wrong?" he asked the moment his eyes met mine. "What happened? What did she tell you?"

"Nothing," I stated firmly, silencing any further questions with the sound of my voice.

Gauge stared a moment before moving toward the Indian. Together, we secured the oversized knapsack, Gauge gawking at me the entire time. I took my place behind him on the bike, turning my head to view the community hospital as we accelerated through the parking lot. There, at the front door, was Dr. Hembold, her face pinched, her lips suctioned into a disapproving scowl, her magnified eyes obvious in their condemnation. I turned forward, resting my head against Gauge's back, certain she would see.

I didn't think as we sailed onto the highway, a sign listing Los Angeles as less than 120 miles away. My heart beat easy, its rhythm finding sync with Gauge's. In the stillness of my thoughts, I could hear my inner voice clearly, its wave of warnings washing over me like an incoming tide.

***

OUR FIRST FULL DAY in Los Angeles was like a dream. We had rented a small motel room for the week, just below Hollywood Hills, the iconic Hollywood sign dominating the hillside above us. The motel was old and small, but obscenely charming.

An older couple owned and operated the building. Both tended to the guests as family, their care and concern for each person a warm and welcome experience.

Gauge was eager to explore the city, but my health was struggling.

Gauge didn't know it, but I was not holding anything down. Just as before, even water slipped through my system as quickly as it would through a mesh stocking.

On the third night, he found me nearly unconscious next to the toilet.

I dreaded yet another hospital visit, but I knew I didn't have much choice. Glimpsing myself in the mirror, I was shocked at how gaunt and thin I appeared. My usual healthy glow had faded into a dim lifelessness, as though I were merely walking skin and bones.

Gauge sat beside me as we waited our turn in the emergency room.

Unlike Barstow Community Hospital, the UCLA Medical Center Emergency Room was grand and elaborate, a multicolored sea of people filling each seat like a carefully constructed quilt.

Gauge had to help me to the examining room once my name was finally called.

"Hmm," the nurse mumbled to herself as she took my vitals. I noticed she changed rubber gloves after every time she touched me.

She left the room without saying a word, scribbling rapidly over a clipboard.

It was nearly another half an hour before the doctor finally appeared.

"What seems to be the problem?' the man questioned before even gazing up at me. He flipped through the forms on the clipboard as if in a methodical trance.

"Oh," he said when he finally looked at me. "How long have your symptoms persisted?"

I briefed him on my history, detailing the last few weeks as though describing some grotesque horror flick, amused at how he didn't react to any of it. The doctor examined my ears, nose, and throat, he too switching gloves with each contact.

"So you've been tested for HIV?" he asked, turning his attention back to the clipboard.

"No," I replied. "The hospital I was at before didn't have access to the test yet."

He peered at me over his bifocals, his silver-tinged, neatly combed mane gleaming in the fluorescent lighting.

"We can test you here," he announced, moving his eyes to Gauge.

"Are you his partner?" he asked, his voice stale and emotionless.

"Yes," Gauge choked out, his voice heavy with worry.

"We will test you as well. Have you shown any symptoms?"

Without waiting for a response, the doctor moved to Gauge and began performing the same examination. Gauge sat perfectly still, appearing as though he thought the doctor would somehow harm him if he so much as flinched.

"We see more and more cases every day," the doctor stated as he concluded with Gauge. "I am sure you are both aware of the seriousness of such a diagnosis."

Gauge and I looked at each other, his terrified expression causing my heart to skip.

"Not really," I answered for us both. "I just know it requires a lot of treatment."

The doctor darted his eyes between us, removing his bifocals and wiping his brow.

"There is no cure for AIDS," he responded in a monotone voice. "As of now, it is a deadly virus."

I looked over at Gauge, who remained still and silent. I had never before witnessed him so overcome with fear.

"What does that mean?" I asked, keeping my eyes on Gauge.

The doctor hesitated before laughing nervously.

"It means," he started, replacing his glasses and adjusting his white lab coat, "that if you get it..."

His words trailed into silence, his face now shadowed with concern.

"It means death. Every patient who has entered this hospital with it has not survived."

I didn't react as I watched Gauge's face flood with tears. He wouldn't look at me, though I knew he could sense my eyes staring at him.

"Let's not jump to any conclusions," the doctor added, turning toward the door. "Until the test results come back, there is no confirmation of anything."

I kept my eyes fixed on Gauge, watching as he lowered his head into his hands.

"I will send in the nurse to draw blood from each of you."

I could sense the doctor exiting the room, but I never took my eyes off Gauge. I waited until we were alone before speaking.

"Gauge," I said calmly. "Look at me."

He didn't.

"Gauge!" I said louder. "Look at me!"

Slowly, he lifted his face, his eyes red and swollen from crying.

"This doesn't mean anything," I continued, surprised at the ongoing calmness of my words. "I haven't had the test yet. We don't know anything until we get the results."

Gauge shook his head, his eyes unblinking as he stared at me beneath a worried, furrowed brow.

"The bathhouse," he whispered, his voice cracked and broken by the weight of his tears.

"What?" I questioned, certain I had heard him correctly but completely lost as to why he said it.

"That guy in the bathhouse," he continued, his stare unwavering.

"What about him?" the year-old memory resurfacing within my mind.

"He did this to you."

My head began to shake as I realized the connection he was making. I was a virgin before entering that Fort Lauderdale bathhouse. Gauge was the only person I was ever with sexually, voluntarily speaking. My innocence had been torn from me that dreadful summer day.

"We don't know anything. Until the test comes back, we—"

"I know it," Gauge spoke firmly, his eyes welling with more tears. "I know it, Dustin."

He began to weep, his shoulders heaving from the sudden rush of uncontrolled emotion.

I started to move toward him, when he lifted his head and screamed.

I fell from the examining table, my knees cracking against the cold tile floor like two fragile seashells. I looked up as Gauge fell from his chair and crawled toward me.

"No, no, no," he whispered, his words reminiscent of my mother's similar cry when I confirmed to her that I was gay. "I can't lose you."

I couldn't cry, I could hardly breathe. Instead, I pulled Gauge's face further into my chest, resting my head on his hair.

At last, the prompting of my inner voice became clear. Gauge was right, the attack in the bathhouse had resulted in a silent ghost that haunted the blood-filled chambers of my veins. Despite the absence of medical confirmation, I knew, as well as Gauge, that nothing in our world would ever be the same.

III.

WINTER

1984

WATCHED AS THE MORNING SUN SLIPPED THROUGH THE SMALL opening in the curtain, the sparse décor of the motel room slowly revealing itself in the slow crawl of light. The polished chrome of the Indian, which rested in the corner of the room, began to gleam and glitter in the soft sunlight like abandoned silver rings lost in a barrel of discarded wire.

I looked at Gauge, asleep beside me, his soft, gentle face now becoming lined and creased from worry. The sound of the distant morning traffic as it clogged the streets of Hollywood echoed around the room like tuneless instruments seeking a melody. I turned to the nightstand, a collection of pill bottles of all shapes, colors, and sizes littering the surface like a pharmaceutical skyline. It was when I removed one of the bottle caps that I realized the dampness that surrounded me.

Once more, I had wet the bed, an occurrence that seemed to happen more and more. Nearly six months after my diagnosis, I was deteriorating fast.

I had lost count of the amount of times I had been in the hospital. The AIDS ward at UCLA had become such a familiar place to me that I recognized more of the nuances and detail of the rooms there than the motel room we had been renting for months.

Thankfully, the elderly couple who ran and operated the motel had been kind enough to give Gauge a job helping to maintain the place. With the couple becoming more feeble and weak by age, Gauge's youth and vitality were a welcome addition. When he wasn't changing light bulbs or clearing clogged toilets, he was dusting lampshades and scrubbing bathtubs. Gauge was a one-man show, and his labor granted us a free room and a small income.

The cost of my vast array of medications commanded nearly every cent Gauge earned. As of now, there was no effective cure for AIDS, though many in the medical community promised of one on the foreseeable horizon. In the meantime, those affected relied on an array of existing medications for other illnesses, nutritional supplements, and a bit of experimental remedies you heard about through other patients or progressive and unconventional-minded doctors.

Gauge did not test positive. He was routinely tested during each of my ongoing hospital stays, but his blood continued to show no signs of the virus that afflicted mine.

I placed my feet on the floor, the ache of my muscles as they clung weakly to my bones weaving through the fibers of my nervous system like lightning traveling a tree root. My knees popped and cracked as I stood to my full height, the urine-soaked pajamas dripping their excess to the carpet below.

I stared at myself in the mirror as I shuffled my way to the bathroom. My face, once plump with a boyish youth, had suctioned away to the gaunt lifelessness of a cadaver. Sores covered my jawline and neck. Every orifice bled and oozed. Though I ate, what I didn't vomit or immediately shit out wasn't enough to sustain a healthy weight. I was wasting away to nothing, each day revealing another bone, each week detailing the loss of yet more muscle, replacing it with another eczema patch or sporotrichosis blister.

The doctors were horrified yet amazed at the rapid progression of the illness within my system. Given the timeline of my likely exposure, only a year and some months had passed, my immune system was depleting faster than an old tree shedding its leaves at the start of winter.

They were learning that most people's symptoms did not appear until years after exposure, some lasting a decade before succumbing to the virus.

I was not so fortunate. For whatever reason, the disease ravaged through my body the way a forest fire hungrily devours an acreage of trees, leaving behind only the hollowed remnants of what was once vigorous and resilient. In the shadows of the dark room, I appeared in the mirror as some walking skeleton, blackened and charred by the flames of mystery and sickness. I felt like one of the victims of the Black Death as depicted in a Renaissance painting, my body littered with flesh-eating sores, my youth stripped from my bones, leaving only a fragile skeleton to be disposed of in the shallows of the mass graves that collected those of the same fate.

I made it to the toilet just as the contents of my bowels expelled into the water. The churning presence of the liquid I had just sipped to down one of my pills was enough to stimulate and irritate my digestive tract, forcing what lingered at the entrails to evacuate my body without urge or warning. Many times, I failed to make it to the bathroom, forced to crouch beside the bed, leaving a mess that Gauge would dutifully clean, yet a stain that scarred the carpet.

I started to wipe myself when Gauge entered the tiny bathroom.

"You make it?" he asked, his eyes still heavy with sleep.

"Yeah," I whispered, always embarrassed that he had to endure the foul odors that now so often emanated from my body.

"You want to take a bath?" he asked, wiping away the remaining evidence of slumber from his eyes.

I nodded.

I waited as he stripped off his briefs, carefully removed my still-soaked pajamas, and lifted me into the tub. I sat silently with my knees against my chest as the cold water began to fill the space around me, slowly warming as it inched up my thighs.

Gauge sat behind me, allowing his legs to wrap around my body. I closed my eyes as he pulled me toward him, the subtle movement nauseating and painful.

Neither of us spoke as he bathed me, gently tending to each inch and crevasse of my skin. I rested against him, the constant pounding of his heart comforting and peaceful.

The bathtub ritual had become so common and routine that I no longer saw the romantic significance of it. Many of the orderlies and nurses in the AIDS ward refused to touch the patients, leaving many to wallow and suffer in their own filth, most only finding relief by the hands of some fearless family member, friend, or volunteer. The ward administrator allowed Gauge to remain with me during my extended stays as long he promised to feed and change me. Many of the common hospital rules concerning visitors and family members were broken in the ward to accommodate the paranoia and at times downright cruelty of the caregivers. They were willing to allow anyone to do the dirty work of their jobs if it meant not having to come into any form of close contact with those who wasted away before them.

"Have you thought any more about what we talked about?" I asked, my voice dry and hollow from sleep.

Gauge didn't respond.

"I've thought a lot about it, Gauge. It's something I need for you to understand."

"I can't..." his voice broke with emotion. We both remained silent as he continued to rinse my skin, the warm water burning my flesh like lava under the sense perception of my illness-frayed nerves. The skin of my scalp throbbed and ached as he softly washed my hair, each follicle signaling pain from just the touch of Gauge's fingertips.

"Gauge," I continued, using all my strength to summon my voice.

"I can't, Dustin," he whispered. "I can't do that for you."

I had been reading about patients overdosing on sleep medications, the massive doses easing their hearts into an unconscious cardiac arrest, releasing the person of the constant pain of their horrific existence. It was rumored that certain doctors were silently prescribing the medications, fully aware of how they would be used, but turning a blind eye in the hopeless reality of what modern medicine could not provide.

Day in and out at the ward, I saw countless lifeless bodies being transported from their rooms to a makeshift morgue just for AIDS victims. Seconds later, another skeletal soul on the brink of death was wheeled in to take their temporary residence in the newly vacated room. I didn't want to go this way. I didn't want to be just another corpse lying in the AIDS morgue waiting for one of the few mortuaries brave enough to collect my remains.

I heard the sobbing and wailing of those on the verge of dying, many isolated and alone, abandoned by everyone they ever knew to face a lonely passing.

Gauge tried ruthlessly to contact my parents. Despite my father's warmth and acceptance during our phone call from Las Vegas, he now refused to speak to me, breaking down one time on the phone with Gauge before hanging up in sobs. Gauge didn't know that I knew, but I heard him one night during one of his many secret telephone missions. He would often call my parents' home in the middle of the night, hoping the repeated, unexpected late-night intrusion would cause one of them to answer. It worked. Late one night, I heard him on the phone with my mother, her distinctive voice cold and emotionless through the receiver.

"He chose this for himself," she stated. "You can only live so long against God before He sets you right."

Gauge only listened, too stunned to speak.

"Or strikes you down," she concluded, hanging up the phone before Gauge could muster a response.

I watched him as he wept that night, his fear and frustration so palpable that I swore I could taste the salt of his streaming tears as they evaporated into the room around us.

I didn't cry. I didn't even mention to him that I heard the phone call. Instead, I would only smile and nod when he would lie to me that he had heard from my parents, rattling off various details about how they were organizing a trip to LA. He even went as far as to say that they were making the cross-country trek, along with Aunt Mert, the three of them piled into Aunt Mert's giant silver Cadillac and westward bound. Deep down, I think he knew that I knew he was lying. Still, I let him, fulfilling his need to somehow comfort me with fabled tales of the care and concern of those who had abandoned me months ago. I accepted the reality, but I never forced its sharp and stark existence onto Gauge. Pretending that my parents cared that I was wasting away to some incurable disease on the other side of the country somehow eased his anxiety. Who was I to take that from him?

Gauge continued to write Aunt Mert. I would see him up late into the night, feverishly scribbling in his notebook. I never knew if he sent any of the several-page-long letters he scrawled out. Perhaps he only continued to add to the ones he had written previously, journaling or keeping a diary of sorts with everything directed to Aunt Mert. I was too weak to ever try to find them, deciding it was best that he keep his personal thoughts and feelings private within the letters. God knows, I am sure he needed the written therapeutic release.

"Come on," Gauge said softly, snapping me from my thoughts and back to the present. "Let's get you dried and back into bed."

"The bed is wet," I told him, avoiding his eyes in the weight of my shame.

"I know, babe. I already removed the sheets."

I watched as Gauge quickly dressed for work after he had carefully tucked me into the freshly made bed. He kept a stockade of clean bedsheets in the room due to the consistency of my accidents. He would never scoff or scold me, he would simply clean the mess and move on, always tender and caring to avoid hurting my feelings by embarrassing me or making me feel guilty or responsible.

"I'll bring you some soup around lunch," he said, kissing my forehead. "Please try and drink the shake."

I looked over at the blended mixture on the nightstand beside me. My stomach grumbled its disapproval the moment I laid eyes on it.

"I'll try," I promised, knowing I would only sip the drink before succumbing to more fits of diarrhea. It wouldn't be long before I would need another hospital visit to replenish all that continued to be wasted, both from the disease and my lack of eating. Some days, I wouldn't eat at all, only sipping a few mouthfuls of water to avoid complete dehydration.

I drifted off to sleep not long after Gauge left the room, visions of the nearby Pacific waves crashing over the shores of my dreams.

***

"HOW ARE YOU FEELING today, Mr. Thomas?" a doctor I had never seen before asked me. "I hear we need to get some food into you."

I looked at Gauge, who was silently unpacking the various items he had shoved into the knapsack before we raced out of the motel room. I had begun vomiting blood, covering the entire bedspread with a putrid bile that stung my eyes and clogged my throat. It was nearly an hour before Gauge discovered me and loaded us onto the Indian and barreled to the hospital.

"Mr. Paulson," the doctor said to Gauge, fidgeting with one of the tubes in my wrists. "May I have a word with you in the hallway?"

Gauge looked at him suspiciously, nodding his head in agreement after a moment of silent contemplation.

I didn't say a word as I watched the two men disappear into the hallway. Several seconds passed before I heard Gauge yelling in the small distance.

"What the fuck do you mean we can't stay?" I heard him shout. "He will starve to death if we leave!"

There were several more minutes of silence. Finally, after what felt like a short lifetime, Gauge reappeared in the doorway, his head hung as he made his way back to the knapsack. I watched as he began collecting what he had just unloaded, shoving it back into the bag.

"What's the matter?" I asked, summoning every bit of shallow breath inside my lungs to carry my voice.

"We have to go," Gauge replied flatly, keeping his attention on the pack.

"What do you mean?" I croaked, my words labored and breathless. "I can't go home yet. I'm too sick."

"They need the room for someone with insurance," he responded, turning to face me, his eyes filled with tears of frustration. "They said they will rehydrate and feed you, but once stabilized, we have to go."

I lowered my head in shameful understanding. One of the more talkative orderlies had once told me that due to the vast numbers of new patients coming into the ward each day, the hospital was forced to prioritize by severity, often dumping patients who were deemed well enough, relatively speaking, for home care, or those who lacked any form of health insurance. With the sudden increase in AIDS cases, many county hospitals were forced to take in far more patients than they could properly care for, often exhausting an already limited federal funding, and resorting to quietly yet hastily dumping helpless AIDS patients back out onto the streets.

I chose not to exhaust my fledgling reserves of energy in continuing to pursue information. Instead, I lay back deeper into the pillow and allowed the flowing nutrients to seep quietly into my system. Already, the presence of the liquid began to make me feel a bit better. It was awful how a tasteless substance was now something I favored in place of any traditional food. I long ago lost my cravings and appetite, resorting to eating mashed and liquid nourishment in order to continue living. I no longer remembered what a hot pizza tasted like as it pressed upon your tongue during that first bite, or the sweet softness of ice cream as it slid down your throat with its creamy goodness. I could barely taste the bits of food I did eat, my taste buds exhausted by the endless parade of medications and acidic burn of stomach fluids as they coated over my tongue each time I vomited.

There were no joys or pleasures in my living. I simply existed. Each day, another spin of hours zipped by on the clock as I faded in and out of consciousness. Only my moments with Gauge, which usually consisted of baths and feedings, provided me some form of willpower. Apart from Gauge, I felt I had nothing to live for, my interest and care for life beginning to dull and dissipate with each passing day.

"Here," the same doctor announced as he reentered the room. "I wrote down the number to the private hospice I told you about."

Gauge turned around to face the man, begrudgingly taking the paper from his hand.

"It's private, so they will require some money up front, but at least they will have more availability to care for Dustin."

I lifted my eyes toward the ceiling as I felt both men move their gaze over me.

"Keep him comfortable, Mr. Paulson," I heard the doctor say.

There was a long silence before I heard another sound. Finally, Gauge appeared beside me.

"I need to go back to the motel for a bit," he said softly, brushing his hand over my sweat-covered forehead. "I'll be back in a few hours. By then you should be done with the fluids and we can go."

Several questions clamored into my brain, but I was too tired to ask them. I merely nodded and closed my eyes, feeling his lips as they touched mine.

I slipped into unconsciousness as Gauge left the room.

***

THE HOUSE SMELLED OF patchouli oil and sage. The room I was in was small and decorated like a doll house. All the furniture and fixtures were antique, meticulously matched and styled to perfection. It felt as though I had stepped into some classic home décor catalog or storybook description of the home of a wise and gentle grandmother.

It took me three days to get the truth from Gauge on how he was able to pay for me to stay here. He had sold the Indian. After he left me at the ward that day, he telephoned Officer Jenkins and made him an offer. Thrilled, Officer Jenkins accepted, wired Gauge the money, and promised to travel to LA in a month to pick it up.

I threw a fit. I couldn't believe Gauge would ever consider selling the Indian, despite the circumstances. The bike meant the world to him, he put so much time and energy into restoring it. He wouldn't hear of my protests, though. He wanted me in this private facility, so there was no questioning or discussing the details and methods of how he was making that happen.

Gauge was allowed to stay in the room with me. He slept on a peach-colored chaise lounge, a handstitched quilt bundled over him like the fur of a hibernating animal.

The house belonged to an older lesbian couple, Barb and June. Both retired nurses, they operated a successful bed and breakfast, the house an heirloom in June's family, temporarily closing it to host a private hospice. Originally, they operated the cause by way of their personal savings and retirement funds, but due to the increase in patients, they were forced to start asking a fee in order to continue providing the service. Most of the patients were those without health insurance, or those abandoned by family or dumped by the local hospitals. June and Barb tended to the day-to-day tasks while one of their friends, a retired doctor, provided the necessary medical authority.

Unlike the AIDS ward, the home was welcoming and comfortable, the hovering shadow of death nonexistent, though nearby.

What amazed me most was the personal care both women provided. Unlike the nurses and orderlies of the ward, the women were not afraid to touch or even show affection to their patients. Barb would often stroke my hair whenever she tended to me, and June would never leave the room without kissing my cheek.

They both adored Gauge and delighted in his willingness to assist them around the house. They wouldn't allow him to interact much with the other patients, but they certainly had no issue providing a list of household chores and tasks for him to complete each day. Gauge reveled in his work. I think he was looking for a way to show his gratitude toward the ladies, despite the money he had given them on the first day. I didn't ask how much he sold the Indian for. I really didn't want to know. The fact that he sold it broke my heart, and I was determined to arrange that he get it back. Someday soon, when Gauge wasn't nearby, I planned to call Officer Jenkins myself to further explain the situation, if Gauge hadn't already. I couldn't rest knowing the Indian would soon depart from us, its presence and character like that of a beloved friend or family member. I made it my silent prayer and mission to somehow get it back before Officer Jenkins arrived to retrieve it.

"Well, good morning, handsome," Barb said in a singsong voice as she quietly entered the room. "Are we ready for some breakfast?"

I smiled, attempting to lift myself in the bed, but was gently scolded.

"No, no," she commanded. "Wait for me to help you."

I closed my eyes as the robust woman carefully boosted me into a sitting position. Gauge stirred at the commotion, lifting his head off the lounge like a confused puppy.

"Well, hello there, Mr. Handyman," Barb teased. "I left a plate for you in the kitchen. French toast and eggs. There's a fresh pot of coffee on the stove."

I looked down at the tray she brought in. Several fruit slices and a bowl of cereal were set in perfect arrangement. For whatever reason, I was now able to hold down most everything I ate and drank. Something about Barb's home cooking agreed with my system, and I no longer feared immediate expulsion the moment a morsel ventured beyond my lips.

Gauge enjoyed the meals as well. In the week we had been here, I could already see a slight change in his appearance. The thin wariness that had recently cloaked over him was beginning to chip away like dried paint, revealing a fresh glow that even included his long-lost crooked smile. With Barb and June in the picture, Gauge appeared to pause and relax a bit, the constant fear and worry I saw etching over his face seeming to slow and softly fade.

"Thanks, Barb," Gauge replied, tossing aside the quilt, exposing his briefs.

"Well, hey now. No need to show me all that. I haven't had the need for one of those in over thirty-five years."

She laughed to herself, the joyful sound filling the space of the small room like warm sunshine discovering the hidden floor of a forest.

Both Gauge and I smiled in response.

Barb's general chit-chat lasted about ten minutes before she exited the room to tend to her next patient. Gauge appeared from the narrow bathroom door, his fitted jeans gripped over his skin as if painted on. His white work shirt was tucked in, the sleeves rolled high on his arms, exposing the colorful tattoos that decorated his flesh-like personalized paintings. I smiled to myself, realizing how much he resembled the very first time I ever saw him, sweat-covered and beautiful as he dutifully mowed Aunt Mert's lawn. It seemed so long ago now, the sands of time feeling as though they doubled their falling pace with the blackened and foul grip of disease. Each day blended into the next, every sunrise revealing new bumps, bruises, and blisters on my skin, every sunset initiating a terrible night cough that spun inside my lungs like an undying dust devil aggravating the arid desert floor.

"Eat, babe," he directed, moving to the side of the bed for a kiss.

"I will," I promised, allowing the smell of the food to stimulate my limited appetite. Often times, it would take me more than an hour just to finish off less than half of one of the meals Barb provided. I didn't mind it; I had no other place to be, and as long as the food remained in my belly, I didn't care how long it took to get it in there.

I was nearly through with the cereal when June entered the room. Unlike Barb, June was tiny and petite, standing no taller than five foot, her silver hair cut short, her daily attire simple yet colorful. June didn't speak nearly as much as Barb, but when she did, it was best to listen, as the pearls of wisdom that often fell from her mouth were worth more than their weight in precious silver.

"You wanted to see me, hon?" she whispered from the doorway. "Barb told me you had asked for me to come up this morning after Gauge had gone downstairs."

I nodded.

"What is it, love?" the tiny woman asked, pulling a chair up to the bedside.

"I need you to have Dr. Davis get me sleeping pills," I answered in my hoarse and raspy whisper. "A lot of them."

June stared at me quietly, her lips fidgeting as she processed my request.

"Dustin, love," she began, "I think we need to talk about—"

"I have already thought about everything," I interrupted, lifting my broken voice to an audible volume. "This is something important to me. I want to do this."

The woman only stared, her eyes glittered with tears in the soft morning light.

"Have you spoken to Gauge about this?"

"I have," I continued, allowing my eyes to drift toward the window. "He won't hear of it. He refuses to even talk about it."

"That should mean something to you, Dustin," she said softly as she closed her fragile hands over mine.

"He is not the one dying," I responded immediately, my frustration and impatience fueling the faint power of my voice. "I don't want to end up like the others. I saw so many go at the ward. I don't want to end up like that."

June closed her eyes and squeezed my hands tighter. It was several long minutes before she spoke again.

"Very well," she answered. "I will speak to Dr. Davis. Though I must warn you, he will not agree to something like this easily. In fact, he will more than likely just say no."

"Then send him to me. I will ask him myself."

I felt myself shaking as I spoke, a mixture of fear, anger, and exhaustion operating my words and body. I could feel my heart pitter-pattering beneath my twig-like chest, wearily reacting to the sudden surge of adrenaline.

"Okay," she whispered, smiling at me through obvious tears. "I will see that he speaks with you. He will be here later this afternoon."

"Also, I need to make a phone call. I want to call the officer that Gauge sold his motorcycle to. I need to clear up some business with him...but without Gauge knowing."

She continued to smile as she nodded her head in agreement.

"I will bring the phone up when Gauge is in the garden."

I smiled, thanked her, and succumbed to the sleep the small breakfast influenced as my digestion commanded the full reserves of my limited energy.

***

"OFFICER JENKINS, IT'S DUSTIN."

Silence.

"Are you there?"

"Yes," a voice replied. "I'm here, Dustin. I'm just surprised to hear from you is all."

"I need to speak to you regarding the Indian. Gauge shouldn't have sold it to you...or to anyone. I want to talk to you about somehow reversing the deal you guys made."

Again, silence.

"Officer Jenkins?"

"Yes. I'm here, Dustin," the man replied, clearing his throat. "I mean, I don't know how much there is to talk about. Gauge and I came to an agreement, and I've already wired him the cash. He said it was urgent."

"It was," I stated, my voice slowly fading. "I'm sick, Officer Jenkins."

"Oh, I'm sorry to hear. Are you okay?"

I waited a moment before replying, conscious to choose my words carefully but too overcome by weakness to care.

"I'm dying, Officer Jenkins," I replied without emotion. "I have AIDS."

I listened to the man breathe for what must have been several minutes before he finally found a response.

"I am so, so very sorry to hear this, Dustin," he spoke breathlessly, his words thick and coated with raw emotion. "Gauge didn't mention this."

"He wouldn't," I said, the emotionless ice still hovering over my words. "Gauge has yet to fully accept what is happening to me. I think he thought selling the bike and getting me into this private hospice was somehow going to save me."

I could hear Officer Jenkins swallow nervously on the other side of the phone receiver.

"But it won't. There isn't anything that can save me."

I allowed the officer to absorb and process my words before continuing.

"I need you to promise me that after I am gone, you will allow Gauge to return to Barstow to stay with you while he works to save the money to pay you back. The bike was his father's. It means everything to him. I can't be at peace knowing he isn't with the Indian."

I waited for a reply but received only silence.

"The Indian is family, Officer Jenkins. You don't sell family."

There was another long pause before Officer Jenkins finally spoke.

"Of course. I understand," he said gently, his words heavy with sadness. "I will be more than happy to agree to that."

I sighed, a tearless weight lifted from my spirit.

"Thank you," I whispered, "I can't tell you how much this means to me."

"You got it, my friend." I could tell he was crying, the sound of his tears jumping beneath his words like the wheels of his police cruiser whenever it rumbled down a desert dirt road.

"Dustin," he started, taking a moment to collect his full professional composure. "God bless you. May God always bless you."

I hung up the phone, too exhausted to reply.

I sank into the pillow and waited for another wave of meaningless sleep to wash over me.

***

I AWOKE TO THE sound of Dr. Davis entering the room. A tall, handsome gentleman, he wobbled to the bedside, his broken gait a casualty of a botched hip replacement. He wore khaki shorts and a loud and vibrant Hawaiian shirt. His gray beard and hair caught the last fading light of the window as the sun completed its descent behind the neighboring rooftops.

"Dustin. Good to see you awake," he chimed, flashing his brilliant white dentures as he neared me.

"I need your help, Dr. Davis," I whispered. "It's very important."

The old man listened without reaction as I detailed my request. He didn't look at me as he moved his eyes to the window, gliding his fingers over his beard while he ran my words through his brain.

"I cannot agree to assist in this," he stated after several minutes of silence. "It's immoral and it goes against the oath I took and upheld for over forty years. I'm sorry, Dustin, but there is nothing I can do to help."

"My dying is immoral!" I fired back, my voice somehow strong and clear. "I'm only twenty-one years old, Dr. Davis!"

The man peered at me through glassy eyes, a worried heaviness contorting his expression.

"I'm about to leave someone who loves me enough to sell his entire life for me," I continued, my voice remaining clear and audible. "Most people search their entire lifetime for a fraction of what I have with Gauge, yet I have to leave it behind. How is this fair, Dr. Davis? Where is the morality in this? What did I do to deserve to die?"

The doctor looked away, tears dripping from his glazed eyes.

"Please," I choked. "Please let me die with a bit of dignity. Please spare me more suffering."

Dr. Davis shook his head, tears running over his beard and dripping onto the bed.

"I can't help you," he replied. "I am sorry, but I just can't."

He turned to leave the room.

"I will say this, dear boy," he continued, his voice warm, yet broken and feeble. "If you decide to do such a thing, please be sure to state your plan in writing. You want to be sure the ladies of the house, or Gauge, even myself, are not to be looked at with suspicion after the fact. It's an awful thing, but I have seen it happen."

He stared at me a long moment, tears still running from his sparkling blue eyes.

"Godspeed, Dustin. In whatever you do, Godspeed."

He turned and left the room before I could respond. There was nothing for me to say anyway. There was only one final option, and it would take every ounce of waning strength I had left to make it happen.

***

I OPENED MY EYES just as Gauge entered the room. His skin glowed in the dim light, sweat, and dirt littering his flesh like dark night clouds over the moonlit sea. I watched as he removed his clothes and walked toward the bathroom.

"Gauge," I whispered, causing him to stop and turn.

"Babe," he smiled, moving to the bedside. "I thought you were sleeping."

"I was, but I need to see you," I said, my whispered tone gentle and childlike.

"What is it, babe?" he asked softly, lowering his face close to mine.

"Will you lie down with me?" I asked, attempting to inch over in the bed to provide him room.

He hesitated a moment, looking around as if seeking some unseen permission.

"Are you sure?" he asked. "I don't want to hurt you."

"Please, just lie with me."

I closed my eyes as he slowly and carefully slid into the bed beside me. The touch of his flesh against mine was cold and painful. My body ached at the slight pressure of his presence, my stomach churned, and my cough reenergized. Every hair along the side of my body that touched him stood in an alarmed arousal, the firing of the nerves below my pores raging and intense as if ignited by flames.

"What is it, babe?" he whispered as I struggled to conceal my physical pain.

"You lied to me," I answered, my lips just inches from his.

"What?" he asked, his brow furrowing in misunderstanding. "What do you mean?"

"You promised you would take me to the Pacific Ocean," I answered, closing my eyes as I spoke.

"Babe," he laughed. "I'll take you as soon as you're better. It's only a few minutes away."

"Take me there tomorrow," I said, opening my eyes to view his face.

He stared at me curiously, the wheels of his brain spinning wildly behind his eyes.

"But, babe, I don't think—"

"Please, Gauge," I continued, closing my eyes again as the pain of the breath that carried my words stung and burned my swollen throat. "Please, just take me."

Again, he only stared, a tornado of emotions spiraling in his frightened gaze.

"Okay," he agreed, resting his head against mine. "If that's what you want, I'll take you."

"Thank you," I whispered, a rare tear falling from one of my eyes.

Gauge never left my side for the rest of the night. He wrapped his arms around me, pulling me close. My skin throbbed and ached in an excruciating response, but I ignored it. Instead, I focused on the gentle beating of his heart, the soft touch of his skin, and the warm breeze of breath that swirled around my neck and into my nose. I fell asleep with the familiar smell of him dominating my senses. Gone was the frailty of my bones, gone the lesions and sores across my flesh, and gone the lingering foulness of my leaking body. All that remained was Gauge, his loving touch easing my spirit, and his protective embrace assuring my soul.

***

WE SLIPPED OUT OF the house before daylight, the soft purple glow of the rising sun faintly illuminating the side of the house where the Indian was stored. Tightly wrapped in a mound of blankets, I rested against the front gate where Gauge had gently placed me while he retrieved the motorcycle. I stared at the dawning sky as the stars began to fade beneath the growing approach of the rising sun. I thought about our first time at the lake and how brilliant the stars were, how I had never seen the heavens so intense and powerful. I thought about our first kiss in the back yard, the memory of Jack Daniel's warming over my dried and cracked lips like an invisible balm. I thought of the first time we made love, how natural and comfortable it was, as though our bodies gave way for our souls to fully reunite as they had done in so many lifetimes before. I flashed back to the miles we had traveled on the back of the Indian, Everglades turning to mountains, grand lakesides morphing into canyons, stretched deserts reaching beyond the horizon. What felt like a thousand lifetimes flickered before my eyes in mere seconds. I turned my head slowly as Gauge appeared from the shadows.

He didn't speak as he propped the Indian on its kickstand and moved toward me. I looked into his eyes as he squatted down, my reflection staring back at me as it had done so many times before.

He scooped me into his arms, my fragile weight causing him no struggle. We boarded the bike, Gauge carefully securing me in front of him. My body screamed and cried its discomfort to my brain as the touch of the cold metal poked my bones through the padding of the blankets. I didn't speak or flinch, closing my eyes as Gauge steadied the Indian and kick-started the familiar growl of the engine. With a final, reassuring alignment, he secured his arm around my waist as he twisted the throttle, moving us into the dawn.

The wind stung my eyes and challenged my lungs as I struggled to breathe as we accelerated from the street and onto the highway. Cars littered the road in sparse numbers as we easily sailed west toward the Pacific.

A woman stared at me curiously as we passed her car, her eyes twisting in fear as she focused her vision. Like a skeleton wrapped in a blanket, I steadied myself in Gauge's firm grip as he twisted the handle tighter, forcing the engine to respond with a deeper grumble and noticeable acceleration.

It wasn't long before the dark blue stretch of the ocean dominated the horizon. The sun began to signal its arrival with a gentle warming as it followed our movement from the east. The highway became a city street that ended at the sands of a beach. Gauge guided the Indian over the soft sugar-white sand and toward the water. I could see distant mountains spilling over the sea in the brilliant rise of the sun. A few bystanders paused to watch as Gauge slowed the engine to a gentle idle, allowing the descent of the sand to pull us to the tame crashing of the waves.

Gauge waited a long moment before cutting the engine. The sound of seagulls screeching overhead replaced the familiar purr of the motor. Carefully, he lowered the kick-stand into the wet sand, assisting the bike as it leaned to the left. Just as the pedal touched the sand, the bike paused, its weight supported by the buried grounding of the stand. As if gripping glass, Gauge lifted me from the Indian and into his arms. I could hear the bystanders scoffing and mumbling amongst themselves as Gauge lowered the blanket from around my head.

"Take it off me," I managed to rasp.

He stared at me before nodding in agreement.

Placing my withered and useless legs onto the beach, he held me in one arm as he untwisted the blanket with the other. I gasped as the cold December air pricked at my skin like formless ice. The smell of the Pacific water stung and cleared my nose as the chilled winds raced into my nostrils.

In a cautious and strategic motion, Gauge lifted me back into his arms, cradling me like an infant. I looked up at him, his face shadowed by the glaring spotlight of the sun.

"Let me feel the water," I said hoarsely, my throat aching and frozen in the cold sea breeze.

Gauge hesitated, his hair blowing wildly with the speed of the wind.

"Gauge, please."

He nodded, slowly sliding his feet until they met the gentle lapping of the waves. Despite the wind, the Pacific was calm and still, as though it were a massive lake. Gauge moved until his ankles were submerged, and then stopped.

With his head now blocking the sun, I could clearly see his face. His eyes overflowed with tears, water soaking his skin as if he had dipped his head in the ocean. I could feel his arms begin to shake under the weight of his emotion.

"Put me in the water," I urged, afraid he might accidently drop me.

"Okay," he slurred through his tears, dropping to his knees.

Immediately, the cold grasp of the Pacific poked at my backside like hundreds of frozen fingers. I closed my eyes as my body adjusted to the extreme change in temperature.

When I opened them, I saw Gauge, his face twisted in sorrow, his eyes closed tight in an attempt to grip his tears. I felt him struggle to breathe as his arms continued to tremble.

"Gauge," I called to him, my voice weak but stern. "Gauge, look at me."

He could only sob, unable to open his eyes.

"Gauge, please, I need you to look at me."

He took in a deep breath, lifting me from the water as he inhaled. I winced as his exhale lowered me back to the edge of the liquid ice.

"Baby," I said as his eyes finally connected with mine. "We made it!"

He smiled, his face swollen and red from the assault of his tears.

"Go get the Indian from Officer Jenkins," I continued, unblinking as I stared into his watery eyes. "I already spoke to him. He agreed to let you stay with him while you work and save up the money to repay him."

His face pinched with confusion.

"Do this for me, Gauge. I can't rest easy until I know you are back with the Indian."

He only stared.

"Okay?" I questioned, my voice shaking as my frail body chilled in the water.

He nodded, closing his eyes to prevent more tears.

"Hey," I shouted, the squalling of the overhead seagulls rivaling my soft voice. "Lower me further."

He opened his eyes and stared, his face frozen and vacant.

"Let me go, Gauge."

He shook his head, water gushing from his resealed eyes. Even with the saltwater surrounding me, I could still taste his tears as they fell across my face.

"Do this for me, baby. Please."

He sobbed, his mouth twisted in agony.

"I love you, Gauge. More than I ever loved anyone. You gave me a life. You made me special. I can never tell you how much you saved me."

He blinked rapidly beneath his tear-heavy lashes and nodded, his body convulsing from his breathless crying.

"I will love you forever," I whispered, seeing my face as it used to look before the illness appearing in the mirror-like reflection of his dark eyes, those mysterious yet gentle eyes I had so easily fallen into that humid summer day on the Florida sidewalk.

"Do it, Gauge. Lower me."

I could feel my body shifting in his arms, the enormity of emotional pain overwhelming his physical control.

"Now, Gauge. Now!"

My voice ceased, and my throat went numb as the icy foam of the sea filled my mouth and covered my face. I opened my eyes, seeing Gauge as he lifted his head toward the sun, his throat tight and vascular in the midst of a wail.

I twisted my fingers into his hand, feeling him grip in response as I steadied my body for one last breath. In the stillness below the surface, I saw a vision of my mother and father, their faces warm and smiling. I inhaled, the salt-heavy rush of the ocean filling my lungs.

The watery image of Gauge above me quieted my mind as I felt myself fade. Feeling the weight of my bones sink into his arms, I closed my eyes and smiled, the flashing memories of the love we shared etching into the tender flesh of my heart as it took its final beat.

January 18, 1985

Aunt Mert,

So, here's the last letter. Sorry for sending so many at once. I guess I just never felt it was time to send them till now. Maybe a part of me was waiting till I could give you a happy ending or something. I know that doesn't make much sense, seeing how sick Dustin was and all, but in a way, it's kinda true now. At least the ending part.

I lost Dustin a month ago. Those nice ladies we were staying with let me bury him in their family plot. They covered the cost of everything. I called Dustin's parents to tell them about the funeral, but they only listened and then hung up. I could never understand how they turned their back on Dustin so easily. He was a good boy. He loved his mom and dad. It broke my heart to see how they just threw him away. I guess in the end, he found peace with it, but it's always bothered me.

I'm back in Barstow. Officer Jenkins is letting me stay with him. I'm apprenticing at Byron's shop again. This time, I hope to make it long enough so I can go to trade school and do it full time. I should have enough money to pay Officer Jenkins back by the end of the spring, but I have a feeling he isn't going to let me pay it in full. He doesn't say too much about what happened, and I never bring it up. I mostly just keep to myself. Every Saturday evening, I ride the Indian out to where Dustin and I camped one time. I stay there all night just talking to him. I really miss him. That boy was my whole world and more.

I feel him with me, though. I swear, sometimes when I'm on the Indian, I can feel his arms wrapped around me and his face pressed tight against my back. I'm sure it's just my imagination, but it feels good, and I like it when it happens.

I'm going to try to come down to see you in the summer. No promises, though. I don't know if the Indian can take another trip that far. I do miss you and want to see you, but I need to stay here for now.

I had my blood checked again, and I'm still not sick. I don't know if I ever will be. It doesn't make sense to me. I don't know why it took my Dustin the way it did. He didn't deserve it, Aunt Mert. No one does. I watched a young, healthy guy waste away to bones.

I would've spent forever with him. I guess in a way, I still will, though he isn't here for me to see or hold anymore. I'll try to go on, but I don't really know how to. I dream about him *every night. I see his cute face and hear him nagging me. I wake up wishing he was there, but he never is. My heart broke when I lost Pop, but it wasn't anything like this. A piece of me is gone now, lost to the Pacific Ocean along with my Dustin.*

Well, I guess I better wrap this up. I need to go fix Officer Jenkins some grub. He pays the light bill, so the least I can do is cook for the guy.

Well, take care of yourself, Aunt Mert. I hope to see you soon. You know I'm not much for talking on the phone, or I'd give you a ring. I promise I will soon, though. In the meantime, I hope you liked my letters and aren't too mad at me for taking so long to send them to you. I'll see you soon.

Love,
Gauge

CRAIG MOODY WAS BORN and raised in Pembroke Pines, Florida, a suburban community that edges the beautiful Florida, Everglades. From an early age, Craig displayed an artistic passion and natural ability as a wordsmith. After several years of pursuing modeling and acting ambitions, Craig has finally returned to the core of his creative soul to heed what he believes is his life's true calling: writing. The result, his debut novel, *The '49 Indian*. Craig currently resides in Fort Lauderdale, Florida, with his boyfriend, Gable, and twenty-one-year-old cockatiel, Alley.